MW00907867

To Air the Laundry

Cindy —
from one teacher
to another!

Krysta MacDonald

To Air the Laundry

A NOVEL

KRYSTA MACDONALD

Copyright © 2019 Krysta MacDonald

All rights reserved. No part of this book may be reproduced in any
form or by any electronic or mechanical means, including
information storage and retrieval systems, without explicit written
permission from the author and publisher, except by reviewers,
who may quote brief passages for reviewing purposes.

ISBN-13: 978-1-7750469-3-6

This book is fictitious. Similarities to real persons, living or dead,
are coincidental and unintended by the author.

Editing by Sharon Umbaug, The Writer's Reader
Front and Back Cover Image by Karen MacDonald
Book Design and Formatting by Krysta MacDonald

Visit krystamacdonald.wixsite.com/website

DEDICATION

For my mother,
and those who've had a mother's hands towards me,
who've pushed and tugged and guided,
who've dried tears and patted my back,
who've handed me pens and paper and books.

And for Brandon.
Because everything is better because of you.

CONTENTS

CHAPTER 1

5:00 am

Sharon gasped, clutching at the edges of the dream before it evaporated into the black of early morning. Albert blew the remembrance further out of reach with each soft snore.

She stared at the ceiling, tiled, painted white. There was a streak, a little darker in one place, a familiar place, where a paintbrush had missed. She stared at it now, attempting to slow the pounding of her heart, thankful her gasping start awake had not disturbed Albert.

She tried to remember the dream before it all was gone, as all dreams go. There had been a bar, loud music. She was supposed to go to the jukebox and play the song. Their song.

And *he* had been there, his dark hair combed back. The last time she'd seen him, he still combed his hair like Elvis. But that was five years ago.

His arm had been pressed against hers, and he'd been wearing a jacket. Or had it been a sweater? That detail was gone. But the feeling of him there, the weight of him, that was still so vivid the molecules in her arm whispered their awareness of him.

Still, had she not seen his hair, his face, his hand on the table with that small white scar below his index finger, she would still have known who was sitting beside her, so close, in her subconscious.

No, not her subconscious. Her imagination.

Her subconscious may have awareness of him. Her imagination was a separate identity. She couldn't be held responsible for whatever her imagination dreamt up while she slumbered.

It was his smell. She would have picked that out anywhere, even in a dream. She remembered sitting in class, one of the only girls in the advanced science classes, and he'd walk by, and she'd know it was him without raising her eyes, without seeing the note he'd drop on her desk, just by his smell. The perfect mixture of the perfect cologne and perfect man, clean and rough around the edges.

Looking back through older eyes, she recognized it as the smell of a man trying too hard. It had reached out and wafted through the air as if from its own volition, beckoning and pulling and wrapping itself around her, around all the girls, maybe. Probably. Definitely. It had tied itself around her senses, around her mind, her heart, and pulled, and choked.

She closed her eyes against the memory.

She hadn't thought of James in years, not really. Maybe a passing thought here and there, a hint, an inkling, but there he was, so realistic, strolling unbidden and unwelcome into her dream.

He had just been sitting there with her, in a booth.

She grasped at the details. She didn't know the specific bar, not that she'd been to many. She didn't know the chipped red plastic table. She didn't know that jukebox. She didn't know the dirty, worn, green carpet beneath her feet. She didn't know the wall beside the kitchen, the huge mirror almost, but not quite, stretching across its length, clouded and streaked. No, really the only thing she knew, in the peculiar way you know about certain things in dreams, was that she hadn't been in that bar before.

But she did know the man sitting beside her at that table. And, moreover, she knew that the two of them were together in this dream. "Together", in all its giggled meanings in the high school hallways, in the locker rooms after the home games, in long walks in the park and in the back seats of cars.

He was not featured in her nighttime imaginings as some acquaintance she happened to run into; no, he was an extension of her existence in that world. He was a part of her life. Not only were they together, but somehow in that dream world, they'd been together, that way, for years. Ever since…

Well, they'd never stopped being together. In this dream world there had never been the argument, the fleeing tail-lights. There had never been the secrets, the others, the decision…

Sharon stretched beneath the bedspread and sheets she had opened at her bridal shower, and willed her heart to slow. *Deep breaths.* She concentrated on the mantra her father used to tell her little sister when she was having a tantrum. "Deep breaths. In through the nose. Out through the mouth. In with the good. Out with the bad. In and out. In and out."

She wanted the dream, the remembrance of it, of James, the remembrance of everything, away from her. Out.

She inhaled through her nose, long and slow, then let it all out in a *woosh* through puckered lips. The sound of "the bad" escaping popped her eyes open wider. She stole a glance at her husband, but he didn't shift, didn't even pause in his even, soft snoring.

Her husband. Her tongue tripped on the title every time she said it. It had only been a few months. Almost a year, actually. Still, other women, friends of hers, gloated with the words "my husband" as soon as the ring was slid on their fingers. Even before, they tried it out. They tied their names all up with the ribbons of their new assumed surnames. Mrs. So-and-so. "He's my husband; I'm his wife."

Not so for Sharon. Her introductions were faltered, stuttered, staccato.

"This is Albert, my... husband."

"Oh? Albert? That's m-my, um, husband."

"What am I doing for the weekend? I have plans with my boy – I mean, my husband."

She had to convince herself to just get used to it. Other people change titles and relationships and names all the time.

The name change. That was the biggest obstacle of all.

How can your entire identity change because of a church and a dress and an aisle?

In. Out. In. Out.

Why was she dreaming of James? She hadn't even thought of him in so long. What was he doing in her dream, sitting so close to her?

She knew the answer, of course, knew that her appointment yesterday was all wrapped up in her nocturnal rememberings. She knew the mirrored wall was some replacement for more austere walls. She knew the green carpet was tied to polished tiles, and the red chipped table was actually a row of simple lined black chairs.

That didn't mean he needed to be there, of course. He didn't need to show up, smelling the way he always did.

Way back when, back in the world of hallways and textbooks and homework and passed notes, she remembered again how he would walk by her desk in class and smile that stupid arrogant smile, and she would inhale the scent of him, the nearness of him.

Her in-and-out mantra hitched with the remembrance.

So what was he doing, sitting near her in some bar in some nocturnal imagining, like he had any right to be that close at all? Not after everything, not after the way he said the words that ended up being goodbye, not after the shrug of his shoulders, the retreat into himself. Not after he left her like that.

She remembered that last argument, sitting on a bench in the park where they used to chat and hold hands and make out. He was telling her she was a coward. She was calling him the same, but they were on two opposing sides. How could both sides of the same coin be cowardly? Perhaps it was the coin itself that was the coward. The decision, the situation…

It was her life, so who the hell did he think he was, telling her how she should live it? No one had any right to do that. She glanced at Albert. Well, she supposed there was that whole "love, honour and obey" thing. Not that she was entirely sure about that particular aspect, either. But at any rate, that didn't apply to James; he'd given up any claim to any decision she made way back then.

But he thought his opinion would matter, that he had a right to her choices. Just because he'd taken something from her, something she'd been taught to save. Just because he had some piece of her no one else did. Just because he'd held her and kissed her and loved her.

He was going off to live his life, to have adventures, experiences. She was tempted to do the same, but she wouldn't. Of course she wouldn't

And then she couldn't.

And yet he'd had the nerve to suggest his own ideas for what she should do…

Well, that was so long ago.

Sharon stared, unblinking. The streak on the ceiling was where the paint hadn't dried quite evenly the last time the previous owners had touched it up. It was just a little darker than the rest of the ceiling. You could only tell in the right light, if you were lying flat on your back, staring straight at it. It almost matched, almost fit, but if you looked closely, if you let your eyes adjust to the whiteness of it, then forever after it stuck out to you, as stark a contrast to the rest of the ceiling as though it were painted in red.

How can something that happened so long ago be so fresh in her mind this night? It must be the dizzying effect of not enough sleep and one too many dreams.

If only she could go back to sleep.

But she couldn't dream of him again. No.

What was the damn song? She was supposed to request it, to play it on the jukebox. She didn't know how she knew that was her task in the dream; she just knew it. Had James asked her to? No, not asked. James did not ask. He told. He expected.

Why couldn't she remember the song?

She ran through the options in her mind. What songs were even popular back in her junior and senior years? There were the protest songs, of course, crying for peace, and the love songs, telling the girls to be true, and the ones that got them all up and dancing when they came on the jukebox.

It wasn't that long ago in the grand scheme of things, she knew, though she felt as removed from it as though she never lived it at all. Far removed, but could remember every detail of everything else, like some vivid movie, the rolls of film stuck together and lapping and ticking through the projector in her mind.

Except the song.

She hated that she couldn't remember the song. Hated that she remembered at all, hated that she remembered everything else, hated that she dreamt of him at all.

The dream was slipping now, though. The jukebox, seconds ago so clear, fuzzed around the edges. The chipped table, cloudy mirror, red seats, all the details of the bar were gone. All she was left with was the remembrance of the imagining. She couldn't quite remember the textures of the dream, the nuances.

But the song. Her mind reached out, exploring memories for some clue, before it all disappeared.

Nothing.

James. His hair. His eyes. His hands and his smell and the sound of his voice saying her name and that way he seemed to always be heading onto something else, something new, something exciting.

It was good she can't remember the song, Sharon reasoned. She shouldn't remember anything. It disturbed her that she remembered so much.

She folded her hands together on top of her nightgown, beneath the covers. She twisted the simple band around her finger. Simple and smooth and gold, a symbol of eternity or something, the minister had said.

Eternity.

Would she remember what the minister said at her wedding months, years, from now? She couldn't remember a song. Would she remember the words to her wedding ceremony? And if she couldn't remember those words, what of others? Her vows? The lilt and halting fall of his voice when Albert first stammered out, "I love you"? Or his proposal? What else would be lost to time?

7

And why couldn't she go back to sleep?

She tried to empty her mind, visualizing locking all of her thoughts in boxes and filing them away in some storage warehouse, so she wouldn't have to worry about them anymore. Maybe even set fire to those boxes, leave them in ash and dust. Out of sight, out of mind. Even figuratively.

She could do this; she could sleep.

How about counting sheep? *One. Two. Three. Four. Five. Six. Seven...*

Albert's snore stuttered and snorted, then fell back into its regular rhythm.

Sharon blinked into the darkness. She listened to the ebb and flow of the grating. In and out. In and out. She tried to match her own breathing to Albert's.

She was not successful.

CHAPTER 2

6:00 am

Sharon watched the shadows slide across the tiled ceiling, dancing with the light filtering through the curtains. She did the calculations. If she fell asleep right this moment, she would still get another sixty minutes. Well, fifty-nine minutes, forty-five seconds. Forty-four seconds.

Forty-three seconds.

Albert snorted, sighed, and rolled his head away from her.

Fifty-eight minutes.

Or she could get up, go dig out the pamphlets she had tucked into the hallway closet, and study.

She hadn't flipped through the notebook and pamphlets in weeks. Maybe months, if she was entirely honest. The last time she had, she'd fanned through the pages, opening to one, then the other, but never reading, never even considering the images and diagrams and captions. Not even the headings.

There was the one with the smiling woman on the cover, her white dress and white cap were starched and bleached to the colour of snow and innocence and the pearls Sharon wore at her wedding. Then there was the blue book, the descriptions inside explaining the importance of hand-washing and sterilization and propriety. Images of little glass bottles and long thin needles boasted the "best of healthcare advancement". There was one section dedicated entirely to the correct way to make a bed, with two flat sheets, mitered corners, and the opening of the pillowcase away from the door.

It was followed by a much shorter section outlining the symptoms of polio.

Though she'd just glanced at the pages, she was able to recite the list to the pace of Albert's snores. Fever... in... sore throat... out... headache... in... fatigue... out... back pain... in...neck pain... out...arm stiffness... in... leg stiffness... out... muscle spasms...in...

Albert's breath hitched in a snort, interrupting the litany running through Sharon's mind.

She blinked away her memories of classes and peers, lectures and rounds and charts, the feel of a pencil behind her ear, clutched in her hand.

She only held a pencil now when she made grocery lists, she realized, and blinked away that thought, too.

She hadn't returned to nursing school since the wedding. In truth, she'd barely attended in the weeks leading up to it. There hadn't seemed to be much point. Once she'd nodded her consent at the blushing, flustered man sitting next to her in that battered old car, her future seemed as solid as the road beneath their wheels, as continuous as the gold band now circling the fourth finger on her left hand.

As real as unwelcome dreams and unopened books.

She glanced at the clock again. Fifty-four minutes, seventeen seconds. Sixteen seconds. Fifteen seconds.

It all seemed so simple. You got married and settled down. *Settled.* You didn't worry about your classes or possible professions. You didn't worry about the grocery money or sitting for the boards or emptying bedpans. You didn't worry about a man's hand on your knee, or the possibility of children. You didn't worry about bars and chipped tables and songs on the jukebox. You just shoved your old identity aside and hoisted up a new one – *Mrs.* – and moved on. Your future was assured. You didn't have to wonder.

You settled.

Sharon turned her head, watching the rise and fall of her husband's chest. He would wake up soon, the same way he did every day, staggering out of bed, wincing at the hallway light as he stumbled to the pale blue bathroom. She always preferred the light green sink and tub and toilet; there was something about the word *avocado* that seemed exotic and modern and exciting. But this house had the blue fixtures, which Albert preferred anyway. So every morning he stumbled into a pale blue bathroom, where he relieved himself in a pale blue toilet and wrapped himself in a dark blue robe before coming into the kitchen. There she'd hand him his cup of black coffee.

At least that wasn't blue.

He'd gulp down three swallows, then set the cup in front of his chair at the head of the small table in the middle of their kitchen. He'd shuffle away to get dressed and ready for work, and she'd slide his cup aside, and set him quietly until a glass half-filled with milk. White milk. Snow and innocence and the pearls she wore at her wedding

The kitchen also came with the house, but the table, that she'd picked out. It had been a present from Albert, his wedding gift to her as a matter of fact, and was round, with a hard plastic top.

"Easy to keep clean," he'd nodded when she pointed at it in the furniture showroom.

"Oh. Yes." She hadn't even thought of that consideration until he pointed it out. Her eyes slid down the single sleek steel leg in the center, the shine and glow and gloss of the tabletop.

She saw lustrousness and modernity. He saw practicality.

She supposed it didn't matter, either way, since in the end the table was sitting in their kitchen, set every morning with that glass half-filled of milk. The table matched the milk, was just as white, just as smooth and shiny as snow crystals. And innocence.

And the pearls she wore at their wedding.

After she set out the milk and cutlery, the sound of him humming every morning signalled that he was almost done dressing. He would hum as he popped his collar to glide his tie across the crisp material, and by the time he was tightening the knot and pulling it up to his throat, the monotone melody would be clear to Sharon, who would use it as her cue to plate his breakfast and top his cup with fresh coffee.

It was only fifty minutes, thirty-two seconds until they started this procedure, the same as every morning. A procedure, like the ones mentioned in those books and pamphlets.

No, she thought again, looking at the shadows and the light on the ceiling. It wasn't a procedure. Oh, it was clinical, yes, but not a procedure. It was a dance. A dance they both knew the steps to, like the ones in those movies she'd seen, set in the days of grand orchestras in grand ballrooms. He bows, you turn, you step left and he steps right and you come together and turn and move apart and come together again, always in your own spheres, always focusing on your own steps, but still coming together to perform the dance.

Twenty-one seconds. Twenty seconds. Fifty minutes, seventeen seconds before she began the dance, before she would step out of bed and start preparing his eggs and bacon or pancakes or oatmeal, or whatever she would be making him when he came in for those first gulps of coffee. Three.

She sighed. Closed her eyes. Opened them again.

Her hands pressed against her stomach, palms lying flat and stretching toward each other, thumbs and index fingers forming a triangle, gold band glinting even in the darkness.

She closed her eyes again, remembering her dream, remembering the bar and the music and the nearness of James. Her lashes fluttered, her breath quickened.

She didn't want to dream of him. She never wanted to. She'd worked to hide all thoughts, all proof of him, and she had no desire to have his presence reappear now, when she was supposed to be a happy, settled-down almost newlywed.

She pushed down the dream, the song she couldn't remember, James' smirk, his hand on her knee, his whisper in her ear, the echoes, the suggestions of the words that flew between them at the end, right before she woke up. She willed herself, instead, to think of the man stretched out beside her, and tried to decide what to make him for breakfast.

Turning away from Albert, Sharon opened her eyes again, staring at the ticking hands of the alarm, wondering at that name: *hands*. Why are they hands? Why not arms? They do not open and close like hands; they are arms, stretching out, trying to reach the little black numbers etched in the face, always reaching, never quite grasping. Everything just beyond their stretch.

Forty-seven minutes, twelve seconds.

She screwed her eyes shut even tighter. Lying in bed clearly wasn't helping her keep her mind focused. Could she shut out the distractions? The thoughts? The dream?

13

No. It wasn't working.

Albert shifted beside her, but she saw nothing but the black behind her eyelids. *He's a good guy*, her mind nagged at her. *He doesn't deserve to have you lying here dreaming of another man.*

Not that she could control that, of course.

But there was some guilt lurking in her consciousness, something that brought up the face and the hair and the scent of her ex-boyfriend, her first heartache.

She'd tell Albert today. This thing weighing on her, weighing inside her… she should tell him. Not the big secret of course. She couldn't even admit that to herself, let alone to this man who shared her bed and his name.

But he deserved to know something.

And she deserved a dreamless night.

She sighed and opened her eyes, slipped out from beneath the covers, settling her feet on the cool floor. She pulled the covers back up to cover the spot she vacated, the corner of her mouth twitching at Albert's nocturnal murmurs. She stepped into the pink slippers he'd given her last Christmas and pulled on the matching robe that waited on the hook by the door, tying its belt around her waist as she tiptoed out of the room. She eased the door closed behind her, one hand steadying it, slowing it, quieting it as it clicked shut.

The hallway was dark, the window in the kitchen the only source of the soft light seeping towards her. She let it guide her. She didn't even pause at the closet holding her books and pamphlets, determined to start the coffee and plan a good breakfast for her husband.

Determined to be a good wife.

CHAPTER 3

7:00 am

Sharon would be just climbing out of bed if James hadn't disturbed her slumber. Instead, she was sitting at the kitchen table, nursing her second cup of black coffee, acknowledging how ridiculous it was for her to be blaming him for showing up in her dreams.

It wasn't even him, she reasoned, but the memory of him. No, that wasn't it either. It was the semblance of a memory of him. She was caught somewhere between *How dare he?* and *Sharon, you're being insane.*

He'd made his choice, and she'd made hers, and now he was no longer welcome in her dreams.

No surprise about him showing up, she supposed. She shut her eyes against the day before, the appointment she wanted to ignore, forget, sweep away from her like crumbs from the table. But she couldn't ignore it, the ache and emptiness, whispering at her about that *other* time…

She shook away the whispers.

The newspaper was spread out before her. Nothing shocking in today's paper. It seemed like only yesterday every paper dripped with details about that King man's assassination. Memphis, was it? Yes, that seemed right. He was shot to death, she remembered that much. Albert told her the details were too upsetting to be concerned about, but she saw enough of the papers and the news to know it was a white sniper. And then, a few months later, when that nice looking young man, the president's brother, Mr. Kennedy, when he was shot, again the newspapers were filled with words like "slain" and "assassinated". Ugly words, words that whispered and hissed with forked tongues. Some of the papers had a picture of the man fighting for his life. Seeing those photographs, Sharon wondered if maybe Albert was right; maybe it was too upsetting.

But there was other news, too. Albert didn't like her reading about the Vietnam fighting. Too upsetting, he said. But there was something about the Olympics, about some American racers with their fists in the air. A lot of fuss about that one. And there was that space show, the one set in the future, she read about that in even her magazines. A white man kissed a black woman, and there it was, right on television for everyone to see. And then of course all the talk of the moon, and those space men up there orbiting it, the astronauts who were supposed to actually land on the moon.

Let the Americans have space, she thought, sipping from her coffee cup. *Just give me quiet news. No assassinations, no space, no war, not even kisses and fists in the air. Just quiet.*

She didn't like those stories anyway. She only saw the headlines, the images, maybe a snippet or two between Albert's waking up and his humming and his food in front of him. She retrieved it from the step or the walk every morning, and then the paper was always laid out for him, waiting, and always he would gather it up and stare at each page over his breakfast. Some days he would take it with him to work. Other days, he'd leave it by his breakfast plate, and she'd refold it, hoping to study it later. Perhaps further study would answer her questions, would add to the little flecks of information she could steal while his bacon and eggs cooked and his bread toasted.

Even when she could study it later, she never felt like she understood the news, the headlines. Those glimpses, those snippets, they weren't enough to understand. There weren't answers in them, or at least not answers that made sense to her; only more questions.

In May, though, there was an article she understood perfectly well. It was right there on the front page in huge letters. Despite all its numbers, its facts and figures, despite not knowing all the specifics of the history of the Criminal Code, she knew what Bill C-150 meant.

Bill C-150. One hundred fifty. One hundred and fifty. One. Five. Zero.

She mouthed the words, now, against her coffee cup and let her eyes wander across the pages spread before her. Nothing like that in the paper this morning, of course.

That had been weeks ago, though, and despite the fears of so many men and yes, women, too, the world had not yet collapsed just because it was a little miniscule bit easier for women to not have babies. Families hadn't imploded. There hadn't been lineups of women cutting out their insides, there hadn't been crazy relations going on in every house, on every street corner and park bench.

Not that she was aware of, anyway.

She had another sip of coffee and held onto the cup, as she held onto the memory of the first time she saw it in the paper. One. Five. Zero.

She hadn't let on anything to Albert that day, when he came in and read the paper as he always did. She'd watched him more than even usual then, watched him scoff and wrinkle his nose at the headline, shake his head.

"What's the world coming to?" he'd said, and that was, blessedly, that.

Though she didn't remember the song she'd once shared with James, though she didn't remember every exact word the minister said during her wedding ceremony, she did remember everything about that day. She'd been sitting in his chair instead of hers, using her pink oversized mug. She'd been wearing her big robe; she hadn't even taken the time to get dressed before coming down to start breakfast. She'd woken up early that morning, too, but not because of James.

She'd just sat there, staring at the headlines, not even really reading the article, then leaning back, trying to pull herself together to get the meal going before her husband came into the room.

One hundred and fifty.

She remembered it all, the same way others remembered the day they found out about President Kennedy being shot.

Though, to be fair, she remembered that, too. She'd first heard *that* news sitting with James, yes, he'd been there even back then, at Macney's, a little burger place they used to go to once in a while. All the kids went there. Their parents even liked them going there. They liked knowing where their children were.

Sharon and James were just sitting there across from one another in one of the booths, sharing some fries, and someone – Linda Reece, Sharon thought it may have been, recalling blonde hair in pigtails and skirts swishing – came running up, her eyes rimmed in red, nose swollen. She slid in beside her and told them all about the charismatic president and the gunshots through sobs and snorts.

Sharon shook her head, clearing the cobwebs of a nation, a world, rocked. Even here, north of the border, they'd all felt it, all talked about it, all watched the headlines and gossiped in classrooms. But it was years ago, after all. The world had tipped, but it was still spinning.

Her news though, for that's what it felt like in May, *her* news, had tipped the world, shaken it, and then almost, but not quite, corrected it.

She heard Albert's feet hit the floor, a stark contrast to her tiptoeing earlier. There was the tell-tale thud, then the sound of shuffling, stumbling, and then a door closing, water running.

Sharon stood up, angling the paper toward Albert's seat. He wouldn't look at it until he sat down for his breakfast, she knew, but it was better for it to be ready for him than to be sitting in front of her. She pulled down a large mug and filled it, and as she turned to put the coffee pot back on the warmer he cleared his throat and stumbled into the kitchen.

She turned, holding out the mug. "Morning, Albert."

He grunted and nodded, cupping the offered beverage in two hands and raising it to inhale the smell of the roasted beans. "Thanks, honey. Just what I needed." He sipped the coffee and smiled at her. The steam swirling up from the mug melted the hard expression from his face.

Three gulps, then he sat his mug down in front of his chair and left the room.

She turned back to the counter where she cracked three eggs into a bowl. She sprinkled pepper across the surface of the yellow mess, and with a fork swirled the pepper stars into the golden galaxy. She dumped the galaxy into a pan, watching as it bubbled and hardened in the fat from the ham she'd already fried. The edges turned up, turned brown, turned tough.

A galaxy of stars. Men circling the moon, while she helped pepper circle egg yolks.

It wasn't quite the same.

She sighed, and slid the pan off the burner just before it all turned black.

The beginnings of some nameless, hummed tune wound its way down the hall and into the kitchen, so Sharon dished up Albert's plate and plopped it on the table. She moved his mug to the side, angling the handle so it faced him, and filled the cup to just below the brim.

It would be one year week after next. Eleven months. She'd performed this ritual, this dance, every morning for eleven months. How many more mornings would she angle his mug just so? How many more mornings would she stare into the cooking yolks and whites of his morning eggs?

White. Snow and innocence and the pearls she wore at her wedding.

Albert hummed his way into the kitchen, smiling at the breakfast in front of him as he sat down. He reached for his mug, swallowed a mouthful of coffee, then picked up the paper with one hand and his fork with the other.

"Did you wake up early this morning?" He shook the paper once, then stabbed his fork into a piece of ham and lifted it to his mouth.

"A bit.".

"Everything okay?" Even as he asked the question, his eyes drifted down to the newspaper.

She wrapped her hands around her own coffee cup. "Fine. Just woke up early."

But his attention was already on the headlines and articles. "Mmhmm," he mumbled around a mouthful of ham.

She glanced around the kitchen. There was chipped paint on the cupboard near the stove. She made a mental note to touch it up, maybe today, maybe tomorrow, maybe sometime next year or five after that.

Chipped paint.

At least it wasn't a chipped table.

She blinked and sipped her coffee. It'd gotten cold while she made Albert his breakfast, but she slid it from cheek to cheek, and swallowed it anyway, and then another to top it off.

"Anything interesting in the paper this morning?" She set her cup down, but kept holding to it like a lifeline. She was determined to make an effort, to at least try to be a good wife this morning.

"Not really," Albert said, folding it down enough so she could see his face. He smiled, and Sharon was surprised to feel the muscles in her face responding, aligning themselves to grin back at him.

He raised an eyebrow. "You're interested in the news today?"

She couldn't decide if he was teasing, so she shrugged. "Only in the interesting news."

He chuckled and raised the paper again, his smile, then his eyes, hidden behind the paper and print. "Not too much interesting. Crime, economy stuff. Someone writing about those hippies. Apparently they're trying to convert us all now."

Ah, the hippies. That was news she was at least a little interested in, despite Albert's disapproval.

She didn't understand anything much about them. But she still liked the stories, liked the questions. And Albert didn't seem to understand, either. She liked that, too.

"Convert us? How? To what?"

"Buddhism, it says."

"What's that?"

"Don't know. Something Chinese or something. Apparently our lifestyle isn't good enough. They're writing books about it now, trying to convince us all to change our ways or something like that."

"Well, that sounds at least like it's something interesting to read about." There was something exotic about the word. *Buddhism*. The syllables dripped of spices carried on foreign air, of temples and chants and a world so different from the one she knew.

There was a weight in her heart she didn't recognize or understand.

"I suppose. Perhaps." Albert mumbled into his coffee cup.

Sharon bit her lip. She could tell him now, could spit it out. There wouldn't be time for a long discussion; he had to get to work, after all.

She inhaled. Exhaled. She opened her mouth, imagined forming it around the words: *Darling, I have something to tell you....*

She shifted her attention to Albert. His head was tilted to the side, one hand around his coffee cup, his eyes focused on the pages before him.

She couldn't do it. How could she send him to work like that? She was envious of his day, his interactions, his office with cubicles and clicking keyboards and modern women with styled hair and lunch breaks.

But that didn't mean she wanted to ruin his day.

Aware her mouth was still open, she filled the silence. "What's it like?"

"What? The paper?"

"What the paper says about the hippies and bud-Buddhism."

"Oh." Albert shifted the pages, the rustling stretching out between them as Sharon waited for an answer.

She slid her fingertips along the porcelain of the mug in her hands. Smooth, the last remnants of warmth dissolving with her touch. Everyone had their own fingertips. It proved each person was unique, she supposed. She wondered what was hidden in her fingertips. She'd squinted at them once or twice, little lines and swirls just visible in the bright, direct light of the kitchen.

They sure didn't *look* unique, didn't look like they held anything about her personality or identity or whatever else they were supposed to show.

Or maybe that was all there was to her identity. Barely visible, only in the kitchen.

She coughed, and the sound must have reminded Albert of her presence, her question.

"The paper doesn't say much about them. They're writing books, like I said, all about Buddhism. They say it's a better way to live."

"Is it?"

Albert made a sound somewhere between a scoff and a chuckle, and Sharon dropped her eyes to her now empty cup.

"Don't be silly, dear."

He folded the paper and laid it beside his plate. *Silly*. There was a streak of grease shining across the centre of the plate. Another wedding gift, the pattern chosen with her mother, blue flowers weaving and dancing along the silver-edged rim. His fingers tapped the tablecloth as he laid down his dirty knife and fork.

He looked at her, and she smiled at the blueness of his eyes. She'd never seen the ocean, but she imagined it would hold the same cold depth of Albert's eyes.

23

Not so far off from the same colour as the blue flowers on the plate, when she thought of it.

He'd always been attractive, not so handsome that people turned and stared when he walked down the street, but pleasant-looking. People were drawn to him. There was warmth and attention in the way he carried himself, and a steadiness that people seemed to like. He was solid, like a foundation. But his eyes were startling, almost shocking in the way they didn't quite fit the rest of his face. While the rest of him was open and unassuming, his dark hair brushed back and to the side, forehead broad as his shoulders, his eyes were different. There were flecks of ice in them. The first time Sharon noticed them, sometime after James had driven off, leaving her crying on the street, that was the first time she'd thought there might be romance in her world one day again.

Albert reached over and patted her hand. She eased her grip on the coffee cup, and the corners of her lips twitched.

"Heading to the hospital today?"

Something lurched in her throat. "Yes. Later this morning."

He smiled at her, and she knew he was good to her, knew she was lucky to have a man like him after everything.

"Okay. Have fun."

She didn't bother to correct him on his notion of fun.

"Any big plans after that? What about for the rest of the day?"

She shrugged. "Oh, I'll keep myself busy."

He patted her hand again - *tap, tap* - and she glanced at the difference between his skin and hers.

"Not too busy, though. Don't tire yourself out."

"Of course not," she said, and meant it. How could she possibly tire herself out?

He pushed his chair back and came around the table to stand beside her. He rested his palm on her cheek, brushing a strand of hair back and tucking it behind her ear.

"I'll miss you today," he said, just as he'd said every morning for the past year. *The past eleven months*, she corrected herself.

He bent and kissed her cheek.

"I'll miss you, too." Just as she said every morning in response.

And then he was gone, his tie just so, his hands brushing the sleeves of his blazer, ridding it of dust and hair and wrinkles as he clicked the front door shut behind him.

As always when he left, there was an emptiness in the air, a quiet where there used to be noise, an echo where there used to be substantiality. The house was vacant, as blank as the wall beneath the hook where Albert's hat usually hung, announcing his presence in the house.

Sharon sighed and shifted her focus from the empty cup she'd been holding for so long, to the empty plate at the head of the empty table. She rested her hands on the table, the light from the overhead pendant catching the gold of the band on her finger. She ignored it, rising instead and collecting his plate, cup, and cutlery.

This was her life, she reminded herself. This was – *is*, she corrected – what she chose, what she wanted.

She moved to the sink and ran the water to wash her husband's dishes.

CHAPTER 4

8:00 am

Sharon watched the bubbles and foam in the sink. They were so white. White, like snow and innocence and the pearls she wore at her wedding. She sighed and slid Albert's plate into the sink. She watched it slip under the bubbles.

The little blue flowers that edged the circumference of the plate disappeared, and when they did, she thought of Margot.

Sharon had grown up with a girl named Margot Maynard. One day, sometime between Christmas and spring break in the eleventh grade, Margot disappeared. They hadn't been close; Sharon only noticed the empty desk, two rows over and one seat back, after a full week passed. Then there were the rumours, the whispers behind textbooks and between lockers, the knowing glances and dropped voices when a teacher would walk by. No one knew for sure, of course, at least not at first, but all signs pointed to the obvious: there had been a boy.

Leaving school for a boy wasn't unheard of. Not at all. But usually there was a ring, an announcement in the local paper, a big party. Sharon had even gone to a bridal shower for a friend that same grade eleven year. It wasn't unheard of, but also not common; most girls, even if they sported that ring in high school, still waited until after the graduation ceremony to go through the wedding one. Though few of her friends ever went to college, they still walked across the stage to get their diploma before they walked down the aisle to get their marriage certificate.

But there was no ring on Margot's finger. In fact, no one seemed to even remember her being pinned.

Then more news leaked out. It wasn't a boy after all. At least not just any regular boy. The gossip was that he had long hair, and had actually dropped out of college, in America no less. He'd been at protests, several of them apparently. He'd had his photograph in the paper even, taken at some rally. Though Sharon herself hadn't seen it, others had. They all reported the same thing, that it was him, clear as day, in black and white, indisputable, holding a sign over his head, his mouth gaping open. Stories then emerged of this long-haired young man sharing his opinions sitting at a table at Macney's, gesturing and talking and even shouting once. James even said he saw him there himself once, talking about the war and waving a french fry through the air as though conducting an orchestra, punctuating his points with dabs of ketchup.

Margot had met him, somehow. That part of the story was never entirely clear. Maybe it was Macney's, maybe a friend's, maybe on the street, maybe somewhere else. It didn't matter though, at the end. She had met him, and people had seen them together. And then one day, she was gone. Her mother went to wake her up for school, and she simply hadn't been there. Most of the stories featured her climbing out her bedroom window, and apparently there'd been a note, but the truth of the particulars, though the subject of much discussion in the hallways at school, were never confirmed.

Sharon's parents were nothing but compassionate for "the poor girl's mother". They used the opportunity to remind Sharon of all the dangers of the world. No doubt the girl was now living in sin, out of a van, getting caught up in who knows what.

The girls at school were not much more liberal-minded. They giggled about Margot, surprised that the mousy, petite girl with glasses "had it in her". Whatever "it" was, Sharon wasn't sure. What she *was* sure about was Margot was now and forever a certain "type" of girl, a type to be lamented, to be pitied. Margot, from then on, would be the subject of head shaking and *tsk-tsk*-ing and eyebrow raising and horrible phrases like, "Oh, isn't that a shame."

Sharon plunged her hand into the sink, the plate, and wiped a cloth around its edge, around each blue flower. Then she dipped it back in the suds. She didn't know why she was thinking of Margot Maynard today, didn't know why the sink and running water flowing over the dishes made her wonder about the girl she'd been told to grieve for, as if her disappearance equated to death.

But she did wonder. She wondered where she was today. She didn't imagine she actually *was* dead, though she supposed it was possible.

Sharon thought, moving the plate to the drying rack and reaching back into the hot water for Albert's fork, that Margot probably wasn't dead. Maybe she was traveling around with those hippies. She could even be one of those ones Albert read about in the paper this morning, talking about those books on that other religion, that *Buddhism*. Maybe she was marching down in the States, for rights or peace or equality. She could even be one of those people on the buses. There were whites on those buses, after all, and Sharon never before thought to watch for her former classmate's face on the news.

Sharon pulled the edge of the cloth between the fork's prongs. Or maybe Margot was living in one of those communes, where people all loved each other and slept together and ran around naked and messed around with all those drugs.

The fork clattered into the rack, tapping against the plate. Sharon swirled the cloth around the inside of the mug she'd set in front of her husband's chair that morning. Her thoughts, though, stayed with Margot. She imagined her living in some little apartment, in some huge city. Montreal, perhaps, or Toronto. She pictured her in the States again. Maybe she'd ended up in New York, or even somewhere in California. She might have to climb six flights of stairs every day to get to her one-room apartment, and have huge windows with a fire escape and spread art on huge canvases and smoke cigarettes with musicians and writers. She might still be living in sin, to borrow her parents' phrasing – and here Sharon inserted an image of a long-haired hippie, the kinds she saw on the news or read about the papers – or maybe she was on her own. Or maybe she was even one of those girls who liked other girls.

Sharon's hand paused of its own volition on its way to the towel on the counter. She tried to remember Margot, tried to imagine her holding hands with a girl or dancing with a girl or even kissing a girl. A vague image drifted forward, those glasses, fuzzy brown hair, just a little too short to be fashionable. She'd been friendly, but quiet, and Sharon couldn't remember any close friends to place her with in her imaginings. Her mind started, stuttered, then surged forward. And her hand picked up the towel, once again connected to her thoughts. She dried the plate and set it aside. Table to sink, sink to rack, rack to countertop, countertop to cupboard.

Repeat.

Maybe Margot *was* with a boyfriend, or even a girlfriend. Or maybe she was on her own, independent.

Sharon dried the fork and knife, then both mugs, and put them all away. She pulled the stopper from the sink and listened to the water gurgling down the drain. Outside the window above the sink she could see the neighbour's house, green with light blue, almost white, shutters and trim. It looked like an Easter egg.

What would the view be like outside a big city apartment on the sixth floor? Or the twelfth? A cramped, art-filled apartment. She didn't even know whether or not Margot had liked art, had even taken the class in school as her "creative" option, but it fit her daydream for the apartment to have large canvases leaning against the walls, to have a glass – no, an old coffee mug – sitting by the sink full of used paint brushes, to have colourful fabrics draped from the ceiling, beads hanging in the doors and windows to announce visitors.

Most likely, Sharon knew, Margot was now settled down, far from "ruined" and "grieved", washing her husband's dishes just like her, her younger adventures behind her. Maybe she'd even married the long-haired American. Maybe she had a toddler running around the kitchen and a baby screaming in a high chair. Maybe she lived in an Easter egg house and made her husband's lunch and washed his clothes and laughed with the other ladies in the neighbourhood over coffee about the night she climbed out her window and ran away into some scandalous escapade.

When it all first happened, when Margot disappeared, immorality and disgrace were tied around the event like a ribbon and presented to the world. But Sharon hadn't really paid much attention. She was concerned with herself, her circle of friends and her family and school and James, of course. Always, all through school, there'd been James.

Her James.

She'd joined in the gossip with the others about Margot, the furtive whispers and shocking "what ifs". But then, like all news, the shine lost its lustre and something new replaced it. Only later, the next year, when she faced her own possible scandal, did she blow the dust from her memories of Margot and wonder at her life and her choices.

But then she'd dealt with things the way she had, and Margot disappeared from her thoughts again.

Sharon stopped staring at the Easter egg house, lest her neighbour see her through the window and take it upon herself to come over for tea. She wiped down the counter for the third or fourth time instead, hung the cloth over the faucet, and dried her hands on her apron. She untied it and hung it on the peg on the wall in the kitchen.

Each of them had a peg, had something to hang from it. Albert had his hat hanging by the door. He removed that piece of himself when he came in the house, came home. He took it off and hung it at the door declaring to anyone coming into their house, "This is my home. I'm here."

Sharon had her apron hanging on the kitchen wall by the oven. She kept that piece of her on whenever she was in the kitchen, which seemed most of the time she was in the house. Her peg, her item, was no proud declaration, more a soft murmur, a reminder or suggestion of something that needed doing.

It always seemed to her that each was a symbol of work. When Albert was home, he removed that symbol. When she was

31

home, she put it on. Even over her robe, like this morning, she wore the flowered pattern with yellow trim.

She went into her bedroom to get dressed. There was no use doing housework this morning, and no use studying either.

Or ever, if she was honest.

She made up her mind to go to the hospital, instead. She'd been intending to go later, anyway, as she'd told Albert she would. Some time outside would clear her thoughts, straighten her priorities, and the hospital always put things in perspective.

She dressed and fixed her hair, not bothering to put away the curlers she'd slept in. It wasn't until after she locked the door behind her and was straightening the strap of her handbag over her shoulder that she glanced up and froze. She realized the dress she'd pulled from her closet and slipped on with hardly a thought, with the short sleeves and neat line of fabric buttons, was the exact same shade of green as her neighbour's house.

CHAPTER 5

9:00 am

Sharon could have volunteered to do anything at the hospital. She had some training, was a quick learner, and the patients seemed to like her. The older patients in particular perked up when she came through, and she chatted with them, taking her time to ask about their families or to comment on the weather. She remembered their names and their stories, and they appreciated that about her. In other areas of the hospital, too, she would sit and chat with patients, and she wouldn't flinch or look away from bandages and wounds. She held babies for the new mothers in the maternity wing, commenting on the perfection of each infant to each new mother. She looked straight in the eyes of them all, even the very sick ones who resided in the quietest areas of the building, those areas that had an air of impending sadness and a heady mix of strong-scented flowers and disinfectants. She didn't stare at the floor or ceiling or tubes when she talked to them. She looked straight at each of them, in their eyes, in their smiles. For that, they loved her.

But the place she spent most of her time was also the only place she hated. The children's department, filled with rows of metal beds and crisp white sheets and tears and vomit and not even close to enough toys.

The days she volunteered with the children were the days she looked forward to the most, but also the days she dreaded.

Today was one of those days.

For the most part, she could choose where she spent her time at the hospital. Sometimes the smiling woman at the front desk would ask her to go to a particular area, usually those quiet parts of the hospital no one else visited. Or if a particular patient had gone through a hard procedure or gotten some hard news, his or her name might get mentioned at Sharon's arrival, and she would appear in that room. Sometimes she even helped out the nurses. She made beds, cleaned, recorded information.

But on the days when she felt that nagging in her chest, when the past whispered in her ear and tugged at her nerves, she chose to visit the children's ward. It was both punishment and gift, penance and reward.

She blinked away those thoughts; thinking too much led to remembering, and she was already doing enough of that today.

It was always hard being here, but today was going to be even tougher than usual. After yesterday's appointment, all those things that she'd kept buried were resurfacing. Maybe that's why she needed to be here today. She needed to hurt her heart. She needed to hurt it to heal it.

She steeled herself as her heels clicked down the hallway. She paused only a moment, squaring her shoulders and biting her lip and lifting her chin, before sighing and dragging a light smile to her face.

As soon as she entered the main room, the hum and buzz of children wrapped around her, a warm but itchy blanket. She shifted under the weight of it as a small boy launched himself toward her.

"Mrs. Sharon!"

His pronouncement sparked a tidal wave reaction from the other children. Sharon had just crossed the threshold of the room when she was surrounded by little upturned faces, asking questions, demanding stories, offering dolls and pictures for her nods of approval.

She patted the head of the boy who first called to her. He'd made his way to her side, and pressed himself against her arm as the others bustled and shoved and called her attention.

"Hi Henry." She smiled down at him, his blonde hair wisping across his forehead when he tilted his grinning face up to her.

"You lost a tooth!"

The boy nodded and stuck his tongue in the tiny gap there in his smile, as if to confirm her statement.

"Did you make a wish?"

He shook his head, still smiling, and then grabbed her hand and pulled her toward the center of the room. The throng of children followed.

Sharon once went fishing with her father. She remembered the pull and fight of a fish on the end of the line, that tug to yank it up. The tug of her heart to the base of her throat now, synchronized with the tug from the little boy's hand, reminded her of that day, and she wondered whether it was Henry's eyes or the shake of his blonde hair that hooked into her.

A child was supposed to be excited to hide each lost tooth under his pillow at night, then fling bedding and pillow aside even before rubbing the sleep from his eyes in the morning, looking for a sweet or coin. She knew there weren't the resources at the hospital for sweets and coins for all these children and all their lost teeth. She knew that the gaps in some of the grins were due to illness or injury, not the natural progression past childhood milestones, but that Henry didn't even make a wish pierced something deep in Sharon, hooked into her, and her insides flopped around.

No money under the pillows for lost teeth. No presents under the tree at Christmas. No tree at all. No cake at birthdays. Nothing, unless the children had parents who brought them treats. Even most of those, though, chose to take their little boys and girls out of the hospital, or at least to the lobby or cafeteria, for their celebrations. And so this room was full and empty, regardless of the time of year, regardless of how many children lost how many teeth and made how many wishes.

Or didn't.

She allowed Henry to lead her to the basket in the corner. There were toys there, all donated, all dirty, all so very appreciated. Some of the kids from wealthier families clutched their own dolls and trucks and stuffed bears. The others, the ones whose beds were clearly theirs for days, weeks, months, had adopted favourites from the basket, that they carried around reverently, but yet never hesitated to share, or at least not for less than a moment. There, too, was the small shelf with the donated children's books. The books were Henry's favourites, though Sharon wasn't sure if the boy knew how to read or write more than his name. Or if he knew even that, come to think of it.

Henry stopped pulling her and let her hand drop only when they were in front of the shelf.

"Please pick one, ma'am."

Sharon was unsure who'd taught Henry manners. Though she'd never met them, he must have had parents, parents who cared and spent time with him, parents who had expectations for the proper ways to speak to nice ladies.

So, even though Sharon always responded the same way to this request, he always asked.

"Well now…" She put one hand on her hip and tapped the index finger from the other against her lips. "There are just so many choices!" The lie was part of the routine as well; even Henry, with his wide eyes and grateful etiquettes, had to have known that the small, battered selection on the shelf did not represent "so many choices".

"What to choose… what to choose…" She went on, tapping her finger in a steady rhythm of concentration. "They're all so good…" Another lie, another tap. "Well, I simply don't know how I could ever choose! Perhaps someone who is really smart, who knows a lot about books could help me!"

Right on cue, Henry ducked his head, his cheeks pink.

"But wherever would I find someone who knows about these books? These particular books? Where could I find someone here who knows all about each of these books?" Sharon sighed, and looked around at the children tittering around her. "If only there was someone here who would be able to choose one of them."

A soft snort was muffled behind Henry's hands that seemed to be trying, rather unsuccessfully, to suppress his giggles.

Sharon swept her arms to her side, making a show of seeing the boy near her. "Perhaps you!" She pointed at him. "Henry, do you think you might be able to help me pick a book?"

Henry dropped his hands. His gap-toothed smile spread across the entire width of his face. "Yes, ma'am. I could do that if you like. If it'd help you, I mean." Another giggle. "Thank you, Mrs. Sharon."

Sharon held her palm up, sweeping it across her, and ushering him, toward the shelf, just as she did every time.

He chuckled again and walked to it, just as *he* did every time.

And, just like every time, Henry wiped his hands on the legs of the pyjama bottoms he was wearing before reaching out and tracing the spine of the book on the left. From top to bottom he traced the spine, then bottom to top. Then he moved to the next book and repeated it. Then the next. Each book was approached seriously, studiously, reverently. His eyebrows furrowed and he chewed on his bottom lip. The children stopped giggling and whispering, and waited, hushed, to witness this ritual. Sometimes he slid a book from the shelf, tilted his head to the side, and shuffled it in his hands as though weighing it. Other times he stared at the cover, or ran his fingers over whatever child or animal featured on it. Most times, then, he put the book back, and the other children murmured their agreement or consternation. Then, they quieted again as he moved to another book.

At last, though, he looked up at Sharon, nodded, and grinned. "This one," he said, offering his choice up to her for approval. Though the dialogue and actions were the same every time, the books Henry chose were not.

*   *   *

Once, Sharon asked Henry why he'd made a particular choice. The story that day had been about a ballerina who had to get over a terrible case of stage fright. The book was pink and quite out of Henry's interests of all things vehicular.

"Oh, that wasn't for me," he said. "I picked that one for Debbie."

Debra, a little girl with brown hair badly in need of brushing, was sitting cross-legged near the basket of toys. She spun the doll around and around and around, pirouetting through a stack of blocks.

"That was very nice of you, Henry," Sharon said, still watching the little girl.

"She needed a story today."

"Did she?" Sharon glanced back at the boy, her eyebrow raised. "Did she say that?"

"No ma'am. I just thought she needed a story." He began picking at the hem of his pyjama pants.

Sharon was sure she didn't want the answer, but she asked anyway. "Why do you think she needed a story?"

He shrugged, looked at Sharon, darted his eyes back down, and shrugged again. "Debbie's mommy came. They went away with a nurse, and then Doctor Fullen came back with them. He talked to them, then he went away with Debbie's mommy again. Her mommy came back and her face was all red. Doctor Fullen didn't come back though."

"Oh." It was all Sharon could think to say.

Henry bit his lip, the same way he did when he was trying to choose a book. This time, though, it was as though he was trying to choose whether or not to continue.

He made up his mind. "Debbie said they gave her lots of needles and poked her a lot. She said it hurt sometimes but she didn't cry. I told her that was brave."

"Good for you."

"She cried later though, when her mommy came back with her face all red and she hugged her really tight. Then she cried. I told her that was okay, though."

"That was good, too."

"Mrs. Sharon, sometimes Debbie cries at night. She says she hurts."

Sharon knew that the large room allowed sleeping for all the children under the age of twelve, but the boys were still kept on one side, and the girls the other. For Henry to have heard Debbie crying, she must have been really upset.

And it seemed it was more than one occurrence, more than once had he heard her sniffles and snobs from the other side of the room.

Sharon swallowed something awful that was lodged somewhere in her throat. She breathed deep, and it was her turn to bite her lip. She weighed her words with as much care and consideration as Henry weighed the books he chose at every one of her visits.

"I'm sure the doctors and nurses are trying to help Debbie as much as they can, so she doesn't hurt so much."

"Debbie said her mommy cried."

It was moments like this that sometimes made Sharon dread her days on the children's ward. How can anyone hope to understand things like terrible childhood illnesses that made mommies cry? How can a little boy, his little body fighting its own battle, understand the horrible, tragic, incredible moments, the ones she saw again and again and again? She'd even sat with some parents, mothers in particular, when it all got too much for them, when they needed a handkerchief and a cup of tea, or something stronger, and a moment alone. They talked of their guilt, their conflict. They needed a breath alone, but couldn't stand to leave the ward. They wanted to help, to fix it all, to put a bandage on the wound, to kiss it better, but for too many of them their reality started and ended with those five god-awful words: "There's nothing they can do."

How could she wrap it all up, things she couldn't even begin to comprehend, in words for this little boy to understand?

Sharon breathed deep, held in the air until it burned, then let it out slowly. She looked at Henry, his head still down. "It's okay to cry when you're hurt or sad or upset. Sometimes you just need to cry, and that's okay, too. But once you cry you have to get busy doing something, playing or reading or drawing or even chores, or you spend a long time crying and then your head and your heart hurts."

He nodded, but didn't look up from plucking at the same hem on the same pant leg.

"Even for grown-ups?"

"Even for grown-ups."

"Do you ever cry, Mrs. Sharon?" He was at last looking at her again, but his fingers still picked at his pants. She noticed the fraying threads.

"Sure I do, Henry. Sometimes, when I'm sad or worried or overwhelmed…"

He blinked at her. She realized *overwhelmed* was probably a tad too complicated for him.

"But yes, Henry. Grown-ups cry. Even me."

"Oh." He looked at Debbie, still twirling her doll, then back at Sharon. "Debbie wants to be a ballerina when she's bigger."

Something cold and hard was back in her throat. It blocked Sharon's breath. Her heartbeat echoed in her ears, but she forced herself to nod and smile. For all her words about the acceptability of tears, she didn't want to cry in front of Henry.

"That's why I picked that book. Do you think she liked the story, Mrs. Sharon?"

"I think she loved it."

*   *   *

Today, though, Henry's choice in literature was all for him. Though she didn't know if he'd admit it, since he always insisted he loved all the books the same, Sharon believed his favourite book was about a little red wagon that wanted to grow up to become a big fire truck. It's the one he chose more than any other, and she had several drawings of fire trucks tucked in a folder at home, all outlined in black and coloured in red with thick, dark strokes. Except that one that was yellow. Henry had explained that someone else had the red crayon and he didn't want to take it from them, and he thought yellow was a good colour for a fire truck anyways.

She carried the book to the chair against the back corner, and sat down, arranging her skirt and crossing her legs at the ankles. The children who hadn't already been following and crowding her raced over, and Sharon nodded at a nurse who was checking charts on the foot of the beds, waiting as the boys and girls pushed and clamoured for the best spots on the floor in front of her feet.

Finally, with everyone more or less seated, Sharon smiled down at them. "Settle down, please." They hushed, and a sea of expectant faces turned up to her, eyes wide, mouths hanging slightly agape or filled with a thumb or biting a lip, as Henry was doing again.

"Our story today is…" And Sharon began, holding the book up so they could see the cover. Her voice lilted and paused as she read each familiar word. Though the kids – even the newer ones - had all heard this story time and time again, they studied each picture she showed them, exclaimed at the shocking parts, giggled at the funny parts, and cheered at the end.

They were still celebrating, still clapping over the triumphant happy ending when Sharon felt a tug on her skirt. Henry was sitting next to her, and motioning her nearer.

"Ma'am?"

"Yes, Henry?"

"Thanks." Then he smiled, a big grin that spread all the way across his face, and Sharon had to look away from the gap where his tooth had been.

CHAPTER 6

10:00 am

Sharon made it halfway down the hall before the shaking in her hands and her heart vibrated down to her knees and for fear of fainting, she had to stop. She could still hear the children's voices drifting and trailing after her down the hall, but the fact that she also still saw Henry's grin floating in her vision hinted that perhaps the chatter and laughter wasn't really there, either. She stood in the middle of the hallway, taking measured breaths in and out, the same way she had earlier that morning. *In. Out. In. Out. In. Out.*

Only this time she wasn't lying beside her husband, willing herself back to sleep, longing to forget an unwelcome dream. No, this time she was standing, a statue in the middle of the hall, entirely in the way of the hustle and bustle of a busy hospital. This time she was willing the vision of a little boy with feathery hair and a wide, gap-toothed smile from her mind. This time she was trying to forget…

No. She shook her head. She had made a deal with herself one afternoon not so very long ago that there was no *trying* to forget. There was only forgetting.

She'd promised herself and God that if she made it through, she would move on. Her life was a puzzle upset and spilt all over the floor. She would gather the pieces, snap them all back into place, force them if she had to, until the picture was more or less the same as it had been before.

Before.

She would forget. That was the deal.

But she hadn't forgotten, of course. Hadn't forgotten anything, no matter how she tried. Of course the fever afterward had cast several days in a dense fog, as though a giant hand had tried to erase it all. But her actions and decisions were not light pencil drawings. It was etched in pen, scratched and engraved, and so though the lines and curves were smudged and even faded, it was still there. She could still read it all.

She could still remember it all.

"Deep breaths," she whispered to herself now, and shifted to the side, just enough to get out of the way of a nurse bustling past. The nurse turned her head to look at her and lifted an eyebrow. She slowed, but she didn't stop.

Sharon was near enough the wall now that she could use it to support her, so she did. She was still in the same position she'd been earlier, as though she'd simply paused in her advancement down the hallway. Her hand was on the wall now, but she didn't look at it, paid no attention to her tiled and shaped fingernails, perfect light pink polish, pressing and corrugating against that austere white wall.

She was on a record player, and someone had pulled the arm away so the needle was hanging in the air, useless. She was spinning round and round and round and round. There was no progress. There was no change. There was no music.

She wondered if the hand that moved the arm was the same that tried to erase those feverish days. Or was it some version of her own hand, the same one that shoved the puzzle pieces of her life back together?

Enough with the metaphors, she chided herself. She shook her head a little and closed her eyes. *Everything is confused enough without all that poetic nonsense.*

She could almost picture the expression on her former teacher's face. Mrs. Chrisald taught her English Language Arts in the eleventh and twelfth grade. She was short, almost as wide as she was tall, and younger than a lot of the other teachers in the school, though she dressed older. She remembered Mrs. Chrisald's own hand against the black board, resting there as she read poetry to the class. She remembered her going on and on about analogies and metaphors, and she remembered her shaking her head, chiding Sharon's writing.

"This," she'd say, jabbing a stubby finger on some poem or story Sharon had attempted. "This. This is too much. You're mixing your metaphors. Pick one. Pick one and go with it. Otherwise it doesn't sound like you know what you mean. Just say what you're trying to say."

Well, Sharon *didn't* know what she meant. She didn't know what she was trying to say to herself.

In through the nose, out through the mouth. She concentrated on her breathing. In. Out. In. Out.

Most of the time, the days she volunteered with the children were the source of a conflicted mess of emotions. They were her most rewarding days, days that restored her hope in humanity, in the future, days that gave her purpose. Almost all of her favourite moments in the hospital, almost all of her favourite patients, were from that children's ward.

Those days were also the saddest. Like the day Henry told her about Debbie, or when four-year-old Johnny would not stop crying. He'd broken his leg trying to fly off the roof of his house, insisting he had wings. The broken bone wasn't the problem, but the constant gasping sobs grated and ached at something inside Sharon. Or when a little girl with pigtails spent her birthday throwing up, and when she stopped for a few minutes and the kids all gathered together to sing her "Happy Birthday", she burst into tears and threw up again all over her nightgown.

And then there were the really, really bad days. The days when kids who'd been playing last week were immobile in their beds, when weight dropped off and hair dropped out, when vacant eyes stared from skeletal faces. Or, even worse, when beds, the ones once occupied by long-term boys and girls, were empty.

It was usually on a good day, though, when the memories would come. On the bad days, and the really bad days, and the even worse days, there was work to be done, others to focus on, priorities to be kept in check. But on the good days, there was that *thing* tapping her on the shoulder, whispering in her ear, "Remember me?" And then it would all slam into her and leave her weak-kneed and trembling, focusing on her breathing to make it through.

Or trying too, anyway.

Even to herself she wouldn't – *couldn't* – name it.

Not even back then.

She'd told James first, of course, and he'd said the right things and worn the right expression. And she thought they'd be okay. They'd get married, and it would all be okay in the end.

But it hadn't, of course.

She'd told herself at the time that it was James' fault that it all fell apart. His extra-curricular activities were to blame. That's what she called it, the other girls. She couldn't name that, either.

He'd kept it, kept them, a secret from her all through high school, but then he got lazy. Maybe he thought she wouldn't notice, what with everything going on with her. Maybe he wanted to get caught, to have a way out. Maybe he thought she wouldn't have a choice but to just accept it.

After all, what else could she do?

When she confronted him, he didn't even have the decency to deny anything. She didn't ask details. She didn't want to know who, or when, or where, or how many or how often, and he didn't offer to tell her.

She could still feel the grain of the wood biting into her legs through her cotton skirt. She could still feel the breeze that cooled her skin. She could still hear the children playing on the playground nearby. Their screeches and squeals punctuated his words.

It had been early summer, but a day far too hot for the calendar date, and she'd told him it was too nice of a day to spend arguing.

But it was already too late at that point.

"Miss? Are you okay?" A nurse stood in front of her, startling Sharon from her dangerous slide into memory.

Sharon stiffened, straightening her shoulders and pulling her hand away from the wall as though she just realized it was hot and burning her. She pressed her lips into a thin smile and nodded once, twice.

"Yes. Sorry about that. I must have been daydreaming."

The nurse raised her eyebrows and shifted her weight from one foot to the other. Her chin tilted up, and Sharon mimicked her actions.

"You're quite sure?"

"Yes, yes. Of course." Sharon nodded a third time. "Again, I apologize for being in the way. I get a little caught up in my thoughts sometimes." She pulled her purse strap higher on her shoulder. "Like I said, I was just…"

"Daydreaming?"

"Exactly. Yes. Exactly."

The nurse didn't say anything at first, just kept watching her, and Sharon forced herself to stare back. *In. Out. In. Out. In. Out.*

At last, the nurse shook her head and shrugged. "Well, if you're sure you're okay... You're visiting here?"

"Volunteering. I just came from…." Sharon trailed off, turning her head to nod at back down the hallway, back at Henry and the gap in his smile and the book and the bed that had once belonged to little Debbie who wanted to be a ballerina.

"The children's ward?"

Sharon swallowed. "Yes." She tried again to press her lips into a thin smile. She was quite sure it didn't work.

"Oh." The nurse's eyebrows softened. "That can be tough. Okay." She nodded, looked down the hall, then back at Sharon. Something flicked across her face, some recognition, perhaps, and Sharon wondered if she was one of the nurses who spent time behind the desk down in emergency, taking notes and names and asking questions in those austere walls while patients paced the tiled floor and waiting in those rows of black chairs.

And if she was, had she been there yesterday?

Sharon swallowed, and the nurse pursed her lips, and looked back down at the hall again. She sighed, and nodded once more.

"I have to get back to work. Maybe just take it easy if you can. You don't want to be daydreaming when you're driving or something awful like that." A small smile almost touched the corners of the nurse's lips. "You don't want to end up a patient here, after all."

"Of course not. I mean I will. I'll be careful, I mean. I'm usually not quite so distracted. Just must have been those kids..." Sharon stepped toward the nurse. If she started walking forward, hopefully the nurse would move aside and leave. "Thank you."

The nurse stepped away, and then continued down the hall, back toward the children's area.

Sharon kept walking. One foot in front of the other, in time with her breathing. *Left, right. In, out. Left. In. Right. Out.*

Now that she was moving, she didn't want to stop. Instead, she wanted very much to be away from that conversation, from the children's ward and the hallways and this whole hospital. Away from her memories. She wanted to be at home, in her own chair, with a cup of tea, away from the smells and sights and sounds that sparked this hurt.

She made it down the hall, then the stairs, then the sidewalk, to her car. Once she was in the safety of the glass and the plastic and the metal, she wiped a hand across her face. When she pulled that hand away, she studied the wet remnants of tears streaked across her fingertips.

"Go away," she whispered. "You're not welcome here." She wiped her hand on her skirt. "Just go away."

CHAPTER 7

11:00 am

Sharon went through the motions of driving home, pulling into the driveway, parking the car, and turning off the ignition, refusing to allow her brain to wander into the past. She kept her eyes on the path up to the front of her house, listening to the satisfying click of her heels on the stone and concrete, refusing to acknowledge the neighbor's house that mimicked the colour of her dress. Her peripheral vision registered the flower bed that outlined the front of her own home, and a nagging voice that sounded suspiciously like her mother's reminded her to take better care of the fragile stems and petals growing there.

She pushed away that voice as she did her own, then slid her key into the lock, and went in, closing the door behind her with a click she couldn't have distinguished from her heels.

Everything was clear and clean and perfect, fitting together with clicks and snaps and pops, those same puzzle pieces falling into place.

She kicked off her heels and looked at them, debating leaving them askew on the floor, one on its side, waiting for Albert to trip over them.

Instead she picked them up and ran her thumb over a smear of something – dirt maybe? – from the outside heel. She set the pair side by side in the place left for them on the shelf in the closet, lined up with the other ones, each the same shape and style, in varying shades of taupe and beige and brown and khaki and white and grey and black and navy.

Except the red pair at the end.

There was no danger of there being a smear of dirt or anything else on those shoes, of course. They would have to leave the house for that.

She moved through the house, shifting the glass ashtray on the end table, fluffing a cushion on the couch, refolding the crocheted blanket draped over the chair, arranging the flowers from the vase on the dining room table, straightening the tea towel hanging from the oven door. She took her apron from its hook and snapped it in the air. She fastened it around her neck and waist, then smoothed it over her dress. Preparations made, she went to the bedroom, collecting the hamper that sat in the bottom of their closet. Resting it on her hip, she creaked down the old wooden steps, her feet finding their way, remembering the slivers she got a few months ago when she stepped too close to a chipped edge. While she hadn't fallen, she had limped a day or two after, and had promised Albert she'd at least try to remember to wear shoes inside the house, or slippers, at any rate.

"It's more proper, anyway," he'd said over his plate of meatloaf and mashed potatoes. "What if someone should come to the door and there you are, barefoot, hobbling around from some wood sliver?" And she'd nodded, as she almost always did.

But she still went barefoot. The feel of the wood and floor and concrete and even the grass in the backyard was far better than squeezing her toes into the confines of plastic and leather, potential slivers or no.

Sharon pulled the cord hanging from the lightbulb at the base of the stairs.

She liked to pull it with a little more energy than really necessary, liked the way it swung back and forth, sometimes in front of the light, breaking up the harsh glare, casting shadows across the concrete floor.

She rested the hamper on the ground, bending over it to sort through the shirts and dresses and skirts and pants and slips and tablecloths and napkins. Colours and fabric types, that is what she focused her mind on now. Pushed to the recesses of her mind were any pesky remembrances, any whispers of dreams and wonderings.

She sifted through the hamper to find a missing sock. Sifting. So much of her life was sifting now. Sifting flour to bake. Sifting through the mail to sort. Sifting through coupons before venturing out to get the groceries. Sifting through laundry. Sifting through memories, through whatever thoughts she'd allow herself. Lights and darks, acceptable or pointless.

Laundry started, Sharon kicked the hamper so it bumped against the machine. She'd been more excited than she cared to admit when she saw it, when Albert had it delivered right after their wedding, a gift to make her life a little easier.

"What more could a girl want? she muttered now.

She often talked to herself in the basement. It made it seem less cold. There was life down there when she talked, there was movement when the chain on the light clinked and swayed. She punched the buttons of her demands for the wash cycle, spun the knob, kicked the hamper again, and went upstairs, leaving the light on for her next trip down.

At the kitchen table she leafed through a gardening pamphlet, remembering the clipped, passive tones of that voice outside. Yes, she would take better care of the flowers. Yes, she would plant and weed and tend. *Yes, Mother, yes, Mother.*

The kettle boiled on the stove, and Sharon set about making the tea she'd been looking forward to since the hospital. She'd sit for a few minutes, with the pamphlet and her tea, before returning to the drudgery of her chores.

Tulips. She loved tulips, but it wasn't the right season. Something reminded her to plant the bulbs before the frost next fall, so they'd wake up first in the spring.

Oh well. There's always next year. Or the one after that. Or the one after that.

She didn't know how she knew that. She didn't know when she learned about planting tulips, didn't know who'd taught her. Was the knowledge just acquired, some part of being a woman? Had it been her mother who'd told her? She had no memory of kneeling in the dirt with her mother, of pushing down the bulbs, of dirty hands dusted off. But it must have been her mother, must have been like that. It surely wasn't in any of her school books or medical texts.

Sharon sipped her tea. The warmth settled in her, thawing whatever had been frozen at the hospital. Sometimes that happened, especially on the days with the children.

Sometimes she got to thinking about James, about their fight, about the glow of his tail-lights as he drove away.

About the days and weeks that had followed. About the illness, the fever.

She was better off, really. She knew that immediately. He wasn't the reason why she'd made the decision she had, but it sure helped ease her mind. She couldn't do it alone. It had been early enough. Melinda, her cousin who was in college then, knew someone who knew someone who knew someone. It was expensive, and dangerous, of course, but she'd survived it. The fever had been bad, and she had thought she was dying for a while. Everyone had heard the stories, of course, of the girls who died. Poor girls. Dirty instruments, secret locations. Girls who couldn't go to the doctor after. Then people would know, and that negated the whole purpose. The knowing was worse than the risks. The pain. Even the fear of death weighing down on their shoulders and hearts and stomachs.

She stayed with Melinda, though, in the room near the campus she was renting with a few other girls. They had a landlady, who also acted like a chaperone. Sharon couldn't remember her name just then. It was something solid-sounding, and it suited her. Mrs. Jones, maybe? Brown? Smith? Wilson? She was broad and short and went by "Mrs." at any rate, even though Sharon never saw a "Mr." or a ring. She had an accent of something faint hidden behind her "s" and "k" and "r" sounds. When the fever started, Sharon noticed the accent more.

She'd hid in Melinda's bedroom, at the top of the stairs, covered with every extra blanket Melinda could find. Even some of the girls from Melinda's classes at the college came by with blankets and worried expressions and suggestions for secret remedies whispered behind the closed door.

And, for a while, Sharon did think she was dying.

The glances and head shakes from the girls didn't help, but Melinda reassured her, shoving away anyone who said anything negative, making excuses to Mrs. What's-Her-Name about why her cousin, who was supposed to be visiting for the summer, was never around.

"She'll suspect, won't she?" Fuzziness clung to the edges of Sharon's sight then, but she was pretty sure Melinda had been sitting in the chair at the desk in the corner of the small room.

"Oh, pfft." Melinda made some very unladylike noise in her throat. "It's fine. The old girl's so focused on making sure she gets her meals in, she's not likely to go searching through the rooms. Besides, there some law against getting sick I don't know about? That's all you are. Sick."

"Sick is right." Sharon remembered the world tilting, the fuzziness encroaching on her image of Melinda. She was freezing. "Daddy said people who... who... girls who..." She trailed off, her head sinking into the pillow. She couldn't finish the thought, couldn't say it out loud. It seemed too big, too heavy.

"Oh for goodness sake." Melinda snapped shut the book she'd been holding on her lap. Yes, there had been a book, Sharon was sure of that picture now. "What does dear Uncle John say on the subject?"

Sharon could see her father's scowl, his eyebrows drawn together, lips pressed. He always had said a lot of things, but it was the way he said them that mattered. The way he measured each word on his tongue, then spat it across at whoever he was talking to. The way he pressed his finger onto the table when he was talking, tapping each syllable of each word with a further press, the tip of his finger getting white. The way he slammed his hand or even, sometimes, his fist down to drive his point home, as if he could force goodness and morality by sheer will.

But she couldn't explain any of that to anyone then, not even when she was at her best, and certainly not in the middle of the third day of hiding under a massive stack of blankets, staring at the wall and shivering.

"It's a sin," was all she managed.

"Oh yes, I'm sure it is." Even now Melinda's words reach across the years and snap at Sharon.

She didn't want to remember anything about that whole time, but she could never forget, even through the haze of the fever, the impressive eye roll Melinda pulled off then.

"Let me guess," Melinda had said. "So sinful. Good girls don't do such things. Dishonour. Disgrace. And the ones who get sick and even die have it coming. That's what they deserve."

"Yes."

"Bullshit."

Melinda was the only girl Sharon knew who sounded natural swearing.

"The only sinful thing is the way you had to go about it."

"I guess." Sharon remembered how hard it was to concentrate then. She'd been so sore, so thirsty, so cold.

"Damn straight you guess." Then Melinda started talking about men. Men doctors. Men politicians. Men laws. Sharon slipped out of consciousness, but she felt better knowing Melinda was there, fierce, long-haired Melinda, who was in college of all places, and had told them all the Christmas before that she didn't care if she ever got married. If a man wanted to tag along with her, maybe he could, but she was not in college just to "trap a husband", and her parents and aunts and dear Uncle John could remember that.

Sharon swallowed a gulp of her tea now. She'd let it cool while reminiscing, while giving in to the thoughts that had crowded through her all day. It was still lukewarm though, and she took another drink.

It had been another day or two before the fever had broke. Only at its worst did Sharon actually believe she would die. She cried a few times, for her parents and her friends and James. Quite a bit for James, more than she cared to admit, even now.

She mostly cried for herself if she was honest. There was some regret, sure, but more embarrassment that her parents would have found out.

Knowing was worse than the risks.

If they found her dead, if that landlady found her, she'd have to phone the hospital and the police and her parents, and then they'd know. She made Melinda promise to not tell if she could help it, made her promise to pretend she didn't know anything about it. She didn't want her in trouble, too.

"Cut the gas, Sharon. It'll be fine. You aren't going to die."

"But if I do…"

Sharon knew enough from the rumours, from the headlines and stories, and from her own research in her quest to be a nurse, that it was possible. She could die.

"Go to sleep. I know you're low, but you're getting better already. I promise. And as for the other thing, I can take care of myself. I'm not scared of your folks."

Sharon believed her. She also believed, though, that had Melinda actually lived with her folks, with her father especially, she might be more inclined to be scared. But then Sharon also recognized that her beloved cousin wouldn't be Melinda then, not really, and that thought was too much for her heated brain to wrap itself around, and so she'd shut her eyes and emptied her thoughts as one emptied a waste basket. *Just focus on getting better*, she remembered thinking. *Then no one need find out.*

And that's what happened. She hadn't died, and her parents hadn't found out. Now that it was all done, now that she had Albert and her washing machine and her apron on a hook and a life her parents had no problem talking to their friends about, she didn't see how they'd ever find out about any of it. About the cash she'd paid that doctor, that after-hours appointment, the way her heart had hammered in her chest, the days she thought she would die. The sobbing tears she'd cried.

Melinda was the only person who really knew. The girls from the college, Melinda's friends who'd visited, didn't count. They didn't know her, they didn't know her story or likely even, her name. They were probably, Sharon realized now, looking back, *feminists*.

Her father had his opinions on them, too. It was all tied up with hippies and rebels and "those types of girls", none of which he'd approve of his daughter being, or even knowing. The name, the label, was a curse as bad as any other "f-word" she could think of.

Sharon swallowed the rest of her tea. She bent to pick up the flower pamphlet that she'd just noticed had fallen to the ground and groaned a bit as her stomach flipped and tightened and rolled inside itself.

She hadn't wanted to think of any of this today. She never did. Even now, to herself, sitting in her chair in her house, safe from other eyes and ears, she couldn't admit what actually had happened, what she actually had done.

No one knew. No one but Melinda. Not even Albert.

CHAPTER 8

12:00 pm

Sharon left the clothes in the washing machine. They could wait until after her lunch. She heated up some soup on the stove. Yesterday she'd boiled the chicken bones from their supper the night before, making a thin broth. Last night they'd had just soup and sandwiches.

Albert had commented, of course. He'd taken off his tie and his work jacket, and was wearing a sweater over his shirt. The collar was turned up a little on the left, but Sharon didn't correct it.

"This it for supper, then?" he'd said, looking at the soup she'd been working on, granted off and on, all day.

"And the sandwiches."

"Right. But that's it?"

"Well…"

"Not that it doesn't look good. Smells good, too. I was just hungry today is all. Was expecting something a little more filling."

"You don't want it?"

"Of course I want it. You made it. I'm sure it's delicious. It would just be nice if you remembered not all of us are tiny little girls." He'd winked at her then. "Some of us had a long hard day at the office. I look forward to coming home to you and to having a good meal on the table."

She'd apologized, and he'd complimented the cooking, the soup, and she promised to have more supper ready the next night – tonight – and every night from then on.

Every night.

The leftover soup finished heating, so she ladled a bit into her bowl. The soup had been good, really good, and was even better now, but she would make something more substantial tonight. She'd promised, and was already planning. She thought of a lasagna, but she knew she couldn't make it as well as Albert's mother did, and she didn't really want to have supper criticized two nights in a row.

Albert had actually been rather nice about his comments. He'd even complimented her, after all. She knew he was kind, he just wanted things the way he wanted them. He was always nice. Or at least he seemed that he always tried to be.

Her father wouldn't have reacted the same way.

Not that her mother would ever have served her father soup and sandwiches for supper.

Her mother was one of those wives who seemed perfect at being a wife. It seemed so effortless, watching her. She smelled of earth and flour and soap. She did everything by hand; no fancy washing machine for her, at least not while Sharon was growing up. She scrubbed and cooked and worked. Her hands were chapped and raw, and yet they held and kissed wounds and mended clothing with fine stitches. And every night until she was in high school, they brushed Sharon's hair.

Sometimes her mother sang to her when she worked the tangles from her unruly strands. Other times, she would talk to her. No, that wasn't right. Her mother would talk *with* her. It was the only time she remembered one of her parents talking with her, not at her, not to her. Other than Melinda, only James had done the same.

When she was little, her mother told her stories of princesses locked away in towers or hidden in caves and cottages in the woods. If those princesses were good enough and patient enough, brave knights would appear to save them. As she got older, Sharon helped repeat the familiar stories.

"And then the brave knight rode up on his great steed," her mother would say, easing the brush through Sharon's hair.

"And he was handsome, right?"

"So handsome. And strong and good. And he saw the beautiful princess, and he rode up to her and - "

"And he told her he was searching for her! Right, Mama?"

"Right, dear. He was searching for her. He was there to break the evil witch's curse. And he swung down from his horse - "

"And he took the princess in his arms…"

"And he kissed her, and the spell was broken. So the beautiful princess rode off with the brave knight."

"And they lived happily ever after! Right?"

"Right."

Once, Sharon had not been content with the end of the story. "How do we know, Mama? How do we know they lived happily ever after?"

"We just do. The stories say so."

"Oh."

She must have been nine or ten then. She was old enough to hear shouts, to register the broken glass in the garbage under the sink, to know why her mother sometimes wore darker makeup than usual. She was old enough to see it all, but not old enough to understand it.

"Mama, are you living happily ever after?"

The hairbrush stilled in its pilgrimage down. Just a pause, just a moment. An even younger version of Sharon wouldn't have noticed, let alone remembered.

"Of course, dear." The hairbrush resumed. "I'm living even better than happily ever after." And there her mother's voice changed. It warmed, sang, dripped with honey and music. "I have you. That's better than every happily ever after in every story ever written and ever told."

"Even better than being a beautiful princess in a big castle?"

"Even better than a hundred million of the biggest castles you can ever imagine."

"I can imagine pretty big."

"I know. Even bigger. Even better."

And though Sharon couldn't remember the specifics, she was sure her mother had laid the brush aside and ran her hands, those same chapped, raw hands, down to smooth the ends and tendrils, and then she'd kissed the top of her head, and then she'd left the room, just as she'd done every night before that and for many, many nights after.

*   *   *

She picked up the newspaper Albert had been reading that morning. It was one of the mornings he didn't take it with him, tucked under his arm, and for that, she smiled. She liked to look through it during her lunch. She imagined other ladies, ones without husbands and families, working in the shops and offices and restaurants and schools and hospitals, taking their lunch breaks now, too. Some would be chatting together, but others would be sitting alone, reading magazines and newspapers. Besides, she liked to know what her husband read. Maybe she could talk to him about it tonight. She did that, sometimes. She asked him about a name from some headline, or about a detail in one of the articles. He liked to explain things to her, tilting his head the way he did, looking at her under those big, strong eyebrows, nodding along as she repeated things back to him.

The article about the hippies was right there. It was the first thing she saw. She remembered Albert had said something about the books they were writing, how they were trying to convert them all to some Chinese religion.

"Buddhism." She whispered the word, loving the taste of the exoticism on her tongue. It tasted of spice and a heavy warmth.

She wondered if her father read this same paper, if he'd seen this article. She knew what he'd say to her mother about it. Well, she knew *how*, if not exactly *what*, he'd say anyway. It would be loud, and angry, with his hand slapping the table as punctuation, and her mother would nod and stand at the sink, or maybe sit in her chair, watching him eat, just the way Sharon now watched Albert eat every morning.

At least Albert wasn't loud and angry.

She turned her attention back to the article. It was meant to sound disparaging, of course, but she didn't see what was so bad about the hippies. They wanted peace, that was the big thing, and the article talked a lot about compassion and meditation. That could be something she could ask Albert about. She knew they used some drugs and sat around and talked and thought. As far as she understood it, that's all there was to it.

She shook her head and put the article aside.

Would that be so bad? She had never done drugs, she knew good girls didn't, but the thinking, the sitting around? Wasn't that what her life was like already? Wasn't that how she'd already spent most of her morning? She hadn't *done* anything, she felt. She hadn't accomplished anything. She'd made the bed, but in a few hours it'd be messed up again. She'd made Albert breakfast, as she did every morning, and as she would tomorrow morning. She'd washed dishes and clothing – she reminded herself to get the clothes from the washer as soon as she was done her soup – but she would have to do it all again and again and again this week, let alone next week and the week after. Even volunteering at the hospital; she knew people always talked about that being noble, but did she really help anyone? Did she really make anyone less sick or even happier?

Did she make Albert happier?

Did she make *herself* happier?

She didn't know.

"Rather depressing thinking," she said to her soup spoon. She held it up and stared at her reflection in its bowl. She was smeared, dirty, distorted.

This morning she'd determined to be a good wife, to be cheerful and helpful and pleasant, to try harder and be better. *This is what I wanted*, she reminded herself, settling her spoon against the edge of the bowl. She wanted the puzzle pieces in place. Apron. Washing machine. The house and the tulips and the husband and soup on the stove.

This morning, She'd also determined to tell Albert this morning. Each tick of the clock brought him closer to her, brought that conversation closer. *Darling, I have something to tell you...*

She's lost her appetite.

She got up and dumped the remnants of soup, then rinsed the bowl in the sink. She'd wash it later, when she started preparing supper.

She walked down the steps to the basement again, tensing her feet against the cold concrete at the bottom. The freezer stood against the wall across from the washing machine. It was brand-new, a gift from her in-laws, for all the treats and casseroles and meats she'd be preparing for their son, her husband. She opened it and leaned forward, resting the heavy lid against the top of her head.

She grabbed the first thing her hand touched – ground beef. Okay, then. Beef for supper.

She trudged back up the steps, again leaving the light on. She'd be back right away.

The laundry was still waiting, after all.

The wind had picked up sometime in the morning, and now it shook the tree outside the back window. She passed it when she got to the top of the steps. Summer was just underway, and she was cheered by the glint of the sun on the window.

"Definitely too late for tulips," she said, dropping the package of beef into the sink.

Meatloaf, she decided.

The oak tree outside was her favourite thing about this house, even more than the washing machine. Maybe, after a bit, she'd have her afternoon cup of tea outside, wind or not.

She thought of the hippies, of the images of them from the news reports, of their long hair and crazy clothing and jewelry. Did they ever eat meatloaf? What did they eat? Something exotic, to be sure. Who cooked for them? She couldn't even imagine them tying back their long hair, preparing meatloaf and roasting vegetables, even sitting down to eat together at a table.

She also couldn't imagine why she was thinking about them today. Must have been the article in the paper. Must have been her remembering Margot Maynard. And James.

Must have been her remembering a lot of things.

She bit her lip and stared at the pale brown paper packaging around the meat.

CHAPTER 9

1:00 pm

S haron looked up the word "liberated" once. She'd been looking through the paper, as she did, and had come across it. There was an old dictionary in Albert's office, and though she did not make a habit of trespassing in his domain, as his office was, she did go in there to dust, straighten things, collect the garbage and used glasses, the remnants of scotch and martinis dried or sloshing depending on the last time she'd ventured in. That room seemed to be the only one Albert didn't care was dirty or dusty or cluttered. Perhaps he liked the thin grey layer on the wooden surfaces, liked his fingerprints declaring his presence. Perhaps he resented her wiping away the traces of him, clearing his glasses and papers, artifacts of his *thereness*.

At any rate, one afternoon after reading his paper over her lunch, as she did most every day, as she had today, she armed herself with an old shirt she'd cut into squares, and under the pretense of dusting, went into his study.

There she found the red book, hefty, worn edges discoloured at the corners and bottom. It was kept, as all the books were, in the bookshelves along the wall. The bottom shelves held heavier tomes, mostly reference books from Albert's schooling and business. She had the second shelf from the top for her romance novels.

"Trashy things," Albert said, grinning, an eyebrow raised. He teased her, but still gifted her similar books for Christmas, her birthday, Valentine's Day, just because. Covers with men posed on pirate ships, women looking out of windows by candlelight, passionate embraces posed for all time, mouths not quite kissing.

She rarely read them.

The dictionary was on the second shelf from the bottom. It didn't take her long to flip through the pages and find what she was looking for.

Liberation. Noun. Freedom, especially from imprisonment, slavery, or occupation.

The newspaper talked about women's liberation, about some of the girls who'd worked in the shops and factories and offices who didn't want to go back to the home, who wanted to work. There were interviews in the paper, and despite what Albert and her father and mother said, the women seemed well spoken. They seemed determined.

"I'm married," the article quoted one woman as saying. "And I love and respect my husband. He's a good man, and he is the master of our home. I don't want to be higher than him. But I want to work. I used to work before I got married, and I miss it. My husband doesn't want me to work."

That interview bothered her, rang at something nameless and uncertain in her mind. She ignored it and focused on the rest of the article.

Another woman talked about her mother. "Daddy'd get drinking and Momma couldn't get out of the way fast 'nough most of the time. She wouldn't talk 'bout it, but anytime she spent more than her allowance he'd go after her. Anytime dinner wasn't right. Anytime she asked him a question. Anytime he felt like it. Especially when he was drinking. He broke her arm, threw an ashtray at her once and it cut her all up. And that's supposed to be okay? It's not okay. She married him and they made vows, same as everyone else. Your man's supposed to love and protect you, not bruise you all up."

There were other interviews. Some talked about their friends, themselves. And some talked about their children.

"I want my son growing up in a world where there are women at his work. And they do the same work as him, and he never talks to them the way I've been talked to. Maybe he will one day marry and his wife will have her own money and make her own decisions."

"I have three daughters and one son. I want them all growing up knowing they can love how they want and who they want. The girls can be wives and moms, but they can do other things, too. I'm happy with my life. I just want them to be happy in their lives. They're little ladies, and polite and sweet and smart and pretty. My girls aren't worse than their brother. They aren't less than him."

Less than.

Did she feel "less than" the men she knew?

She doubted Melinda ever felt less than a man. Or, if she did, she doubted she let them know, she doubted she wore that "lesser" status in public.

Did she feel like she needed liberation? Was she imprisoned? Enslaved? Occupied? She hadn't thought of it before.

The cotton squares rested on the arm of the chair. She picked them up, peeled them apart, then restacked them, lining their edges up. After setting them back on the arm of the chair, she ran her fingertips over the top one, smoothing it out.

The article had been so straightforward it had seemed easy, determining right and wrong. She knew home was comfort, love, warmth, and she knew it was a duty, no, a blessing, to be able to provide that for someone she loved. But she read no dismissiveness or malice in the lines in the article. Oh, there was anger, but it wasn't what she'd thought, wasn't what her father and Albert had said about the whole thing either. Their conversations about the types of women the article addressed were peppered with phrases like "should be happy" and "isn't it enough" and "how dare they".

Sharon didn't understand.

Maybe her father and Albert were right about certain things after all. Maybe women didn't know about certain things, couldn't understand about politics and current events.

The dictionary didn't answer her question though, didn't erase that annoying ping at the back of her head when she read about that woman and her son, or the one about her daughters.

These women were supposed to be *against* family, she thought. Yet there in black and white, they were talking about their family members. Their children. And they wanted good things for them.

They didn't seem against family at all. That's what she didn't understand; why she didn't understand.

She slid the stack of dust clothes back and forth over the chair's arm, watching the brown leather disappear and reappear with every swipe. There. Gone. There. Gone.

Then she'd pushed herself up, smoothed her skirt, and heaved the dictionary back in place. She gathered her precise stack of dust cloths, an empty martini glass from the desk, and tiptoed from the room, clicking the door closed behind her.

*   *   *

Sharon shook her head. She didn't know how long she'd been staring into the sink. Too long. She straightened, pushing into the small of her back with her fist, stretching her head first to one side, then the other.

She left the package to thaw, and fixed her attention on her tasks. She needed to stop remembering, stop thinking so much. With so much of the day still stretching out before her, she needed to focus on something other than her rememberings. Her chores would suffice.

It always seemed to work for her all the times before.

She slipped through the door to the basement and back down the creaking steps. She pulled the clothes and linens from the washing machine into a laundry basket.

"One load's enough for today," she told the machine, patting the top of it after she closed the door, as though it was a good dog. She hefted the basket to her hip, and moved to the light, yanking on the cord hard enough that the string snapped up. She went up the stairs in the dark, and slipped on the pair of flat garden shoes she left by the back door. She didn't put the basket down, but ambled through the door sideways. Only when she stepped to the clothesline did she set down the basket, pulling out the bag of clothespins she kept by the line. She held two between her lips, then used her hands to begin hanging Albert's shirts, his shorts, her kitchen towels and napkins.

One by one each item went up, and she pulled on the line to slide garments along. The pulley squeaked with every tug.

"I'll have to get Albert to grease that for me," she said, but between the clothespins the words came out muffled and mumbled, all consonants squeezed out from between wood and lips. *No matter*, she thought. *Who am I talking to anyway?*

The corners of her mouth twitched up in response. She wanted to laugh at herself, at the silliness of a woman standing out in the back yard with clothespins hanging out of her mouth, talking to herself. She didn't though, didn't want to spit out the clothespins.

The towels went up next, the wind pulling at them and whipping them toward the tree. Her smile broadened. The wind would dry the clothes, the towels, quicker. Plus, something about windy days just made laundry smell better.

She took the pins from her mouth and used them on the last of the napkins. She started humming, the lilts and tones matching a popular song she'd heard on the radio in the car on the way to the hospital. She hadn't listened to the anything on the way home, focused as she was only on her breathing that steady in and out rhythm instead of everything else that had crept up on her at the hospital.

But now, hanging these napkins, those shirts, the tune from earlier in the morning was there, something she couldn't remember the title of. Something about a girl waiting for her boy to come home. Something about her loving him, crooning and crying that she'd be true.

Being true, always being true.

She wondered, then, at Albert's humming in the morning. Did those nameless tunes have a source? Were they bits and pieces collected through his days and weeks, like child collecting bits of strings and buttons for their games? Or were they as meaningless as they were nameless?

The wind tugged at her dress and hair, pulling a tendril out and wiping it across her face. She kept humming and tucked it back behind her ear. When she bent to pick up the basket, the wind teased it out again. She rested the basket back on her hip and went inside.

Dropping the basket by the back door, she slipped off her garden shoes, looked at the basket again, and kicked it aside. She went back into the living room.

There was time now, while she waited for Mother Nature to do her work outside. She could organize something, menu plan maybe. She went to the bar cart in the living room. She selected one of the hi-ball glasses and dropped in two ice cubes from the bucket she kept in there. It was always filled, always ready for whenever Albert wanted a drink. The ice clinked in the bottom of the glass, and she lifted the whiskey decanter from the top shelf of the cart, then splashed in just enough of the amber liquid to cover the bottom. She set it back in its place, then topped up the glass with soda. She lifted her glass, the bubbles fizzing up and hissing at the air, and went into the living room.

She thought of her nursing textbooks and pamphlets. She could go get one now and flip through it. She could start studying again.

She'd asked Albert what he thought of that a month or so back, if he'd mind her finishing her studies.

"Why would you want to do that?" He'd been speaking into the darkness in their bedroom. The lights were out, and she was facing the wall.

She bit her lip. How could she explain the weight in her arms of Molly, her favourite doll as a child, that she'd carry to her bed table when she was little? It seemed Molly was always sick, and Sharon would check her temperature, ask her questions, check in her ears and her mouth. She even pretended to operate once, though she hadn't actually harmed the doll. She was too precious to her to cut into and investigate. But she'd pretended. How could she explain it? Explain leaning over that doll, thinking that this, *this* was what she wanted to do.

She said nothing, and wasn't sure if Albert felt the rise and fall of her shoulders.

"I want you to be happy, Sharon. So while I don't see any particular purpose behind it, I don't see any harm in learning things."

She smiled into the dark. "Thank you."

"Of course, my dear. Besides…" Here she heard him shift, felt the mattress depress.

"Besides, it will be good knowledge for you to have for the children."

She breathed deep. "Of course," she'd whispered to the wall.

She took a sip now of her drink and blinked at the fizz.

What was the point of studying now? He allowed her to learn to help his home; he had no interest, she was sure, in her actually becoming a nurse, of her actually working in a hospital.

She had another drink, swallowing more of the barely-coloured liquid. It bubbled down her throat, and she smiled at the sensation, refreshed. She took a bigger drink, a gulp.

Why study?

The article in the paper that morning, the one she was thinking about as she stared into the sink a few minutes ago, had women talking about their families. Some were mothers. She remembered the one talking about her son and their daughters. That stuck out in her memory. At the time she'd thought about that one boy being surrounded by all those girls, thought about how Albert was the only boy in his family, too. But now, looking back, she thought about those girls, about the world they were growing up in.

She took another gulp.

If that was me, what would I want for my girls? The woman in the paper wanted her kids to grow up "knowing they can love how they want and who they want". That seemed a nice sentiment, but Sharon didn't know what it meant. She loved who she wanted and how she wanted, and it didn't get her that much of a different life than her mother or her friends.

Another gulp. When the ice cubes fell back down, they clinked against the bottom of the glass. Sharon got up and moved across to the bar cart again. She ran her finger along the top of the gold painted trim. *Must come polish in here soon. Clean this cart.* She poured herself another drink.

Back in her chair, Sharon drank. Her glass was a little fuller and a little darker than it was before, but she reasoned with the wind hurling itself against the clothes outside, everything would be dry after just this last drink.

Daughters, daughters. She thought of herself as a child, as a teenager. She thought of James, of the back of his car, of her crying. She thought of Albert, good, kind, no-nonsense Albert. She thought of that dress with the lace, of the colour white.

"Snow and innocence and the pearls I wore at my wedding." She whispered the words as a sing-song, smiling at the wall across from her, where a wedding picture hung. She and Albert posed in front of the church.

They had thrown rice at them, and if you knew where to look, and were close enough, you could still see some rice on the ground around them. It had even gotten in her hair, everywhere the veil wasn't covering, it seemed.

It had been a good day, that day. She hadn't been sure if it would be, but it was. She'd want a day like that for her daughter, if she ever had one. She'd want her to be able to look at a picture of herself on her wedding day and smile.

But she wouldn't want her to have to whisper requests across a dark room. She wouldn't want her to have to ask permission to do things, to learn. She wouldn't want her to have to face the wall when she went to bed, rather than the man she married. She wouldn't want her to know the exact order of her husband's morning, know how many times he raised his coffee cup to his lips.

No, wait. Strike that. She smiled again. She would want her daughter to know that. She liked knowing Albert so well, after so short an amount of time. There was something comforting in it. What she didn't like was *why* she knew it. She knew it because she was always watching, always waiting, always observing. She knew it because she knew exactly how to time his coffee, his breakfast, his dishes, his departure. She knew it because she was *supposed* to know it.

That was what she wouldn't want.

She took another gulp, then another, then tilted the glass back and poured the remaining liquid down her throat. She coughed, spurting, burning.

"God, if you can hear me," she whispered when her raw throat cooled, peering down at the ice cubes, one eyebrow raised, "Please just give me sons."

CHAPTER 10

2:00 pm

Sharon hefted herself up, hesitating as she stood, not quite ready to leave the comfort of the chair, the seat, the warmth of the drink. She coughed again, wincing at the rawness. She thought of Molly, of a smaller version of herself asking the plastic doll about a sore throat, staring at her mouth. The corner of Sharon's lips twitched. Of all the various maladies Molly complained of, Sharon couldn't recall one ever being caused by gulping whiskey too fast.

She dragged her feet towards the back door and stood at the screen, watching the wind lift and pull at the clothing hung there. "Probably done now," she muttered.

There was a small hole in the corner of the screen. She blinked at it, making a note to add that repair to Albert's to-do list for the weekend.

She shifted and stood on her tiptoes, so her left eye was on level with the hole. She screwed shut her right eye and peered through the hole, teetering. To keep her balance, she rested one hand on each side of the door. Through that makeshift telescope, she could see the clothesline, the towels and Albert's clothes whipping around, swiping across her vision.

The sound of something chattering and chirping pulled her attention away from the shorts and shirts. At the end of the yard stood two apple trees, their branches reaching well past the white fence that embraced the yard. On one of the branches was a bird. When Sharon focused, she saw it hopping along one of the middle branches, no doubt searching for insects. It would find what it wanted, and then lift itself into the air and move on to the next place, the next goal.

Sharon tilted her head, studying it, considering it.

That bird could live its whole life hopping and flying and flapping, moving from one tree to the next. Or it could settle in, build a nest, have a home, raise little birds that would chirp and cry and wait with gaping mouths for worms and bugs until they got big enough to be shoved off the branches, out of their nests, and out into the air and the sky and the world.

"Poor, silly thing."

Sharon practiced shifting her focus from the tree to the laundry, the branches to the fabric. Tree. Laundry. Tree. Laundry. Tree. Laundry.

Tree.

She sighed, and pushed herself from the door, wobbling backward as she came down on her heels.

She didn't go out to collect the laundry yet, though. Something about the bird irked her, nagged at something within her mind, just past the recesses of consciousness. That nagging *something* had a voice, a whispering voice hissing with the incessantness of her mother but the no-nonsense tone of

Melinda. *What an odd combination.* Was it possible for two more opposite women to exist in the world?

She wanted to be away from the bird, away from the tree and the laundry and the tiny hole in the screen door. She needed something to distract her, so she turned her back on the door and the backyard, and went to the closet with her box of books and pamphlets and manuals.

She knelt on the floor, moving aside the broom to get to the box. She slid it toward her and hefted out the top book, the one with the smiling woman on the cover, her hat starched and bleached white, declaring order and precision and innocence. It was reassuring, that preciseness, that cleanness, she knew. It spoke of a woman who knew how to make a bed just so, who knew what to say to a worried patient, who had calm hands and a kind, straightforward smile, who knew just what to say and just the right tone in which to say it.

She opened the book to a random page in the center. The smiling woman on this page was a sketched illustration, but still her dress was white, her hat was white, even her teeth peeking through her grin were white. She was holding a clipboard, standing over a little boy sitting in a chair.

The image of Henry, sitting in a similar chair, came to mind. But Henry would never sit so still as the boy in this picture. Unless he was hearing a story, any story, Henry was all wiggles and squirms, all questions and comments and "did-you-knows". Still, something about the shaggy hair, the gaping smile, the upturned face, reminded her of the little boy she read to on her best and worst days.

Sharon leaned against the wall and arranged her skirt to fan out so she could sit cross-legged, in a most unladylike fashion.

There was a whole section in this text on modesty and propriety, Sharon remembered. Perhaps she should read that section now.

Instead she lingered on the image of the sketched woman and the little boy, tracing the lines and curves of the two characters, wondering at the words in the white space between them.

The information on this page and the next was about talking to children.

Sharon turned the page. Then the next, letting her eyes slide over the titles and captions and text blocks without reading or comprehending. More images, more smiling faces, more white hats.

She sighed and leaned her head against the wall.

This hadn't worked.

She wasn't distracted.

Instead of a bird hopping along a branch, white hats and wide-eyed children pestered her thoughts, conjecturing and questioning and reminding her of her duties and her hesitations and the overlaps and spaces between those two things.

James thought nursing was great. He told her she'd be so good at it, with her quiet voice and high marks in their classes. He made jokes about her looking after him, taking care of him when he was sick, tucking blankets around him and spooning food towards his drooling mouth when they got old. She laughed then, smacking his arm and throwing her head back, and he'd dip his head and chuckle, then tell her, dropping his voice, how pretty her neck was, how her eyes shone when she laughed, and how cute she was when she blushed, as she always did to his compliments.

His compliments were always like that, focused on her eyes, her smile, her neck, her face. Always her looks. Always physical.

Other times, he'd hold up his arm. "Nurse Sharon, I have a boo-boo. Want to kiss it better?" And she'd laugh and drop a peck to the spot he pointed to.

"And here," he'd add, point to his elbow maybe, or his hand, or his wrist. And again, she'd press her smirking lips to the affected spot. "And here." He'd point to his cheek. "And here," he'd add one last time, always pointing to his mouth.

She smiled now at the memory, a soft smile, not quite enough to dimple her cheeks.

She remembered his cheek. They were young enough that he didn't have to shave every day, or even every other day, and there was sometimes rough stubble on his cheeks that chafed her lips. She commented on it once, and he'd asked if there were tips for chafed lips in her books. Then he tapped the tip of her nose up with his index finger, and grinned at her blinking reaction.

She wasn't sure why she remembered that now, that tap, that grin, that stubbly cheek. "Must be that dream," she thought, and dropped her hand to her stomach. The dream, the hospital, Henry, Albert.

Even the damn bird hopping around outside.

"Just one of those days, I guess." She studied the crease where the wall met the ceiling.

"I'm making a regular habit of talking to myself, it seems." She smoothed the green fabric of her dress without shifting her attention. "After only a year. I can't imagine the conversations I'll have with myself after a few years." She closed her eyes. "Or after fifty years."

That thought pulled at her, and she shook her head, messing the back of her hair against the wall.

"No good thinking of that now," she said to the crease in the ceiling.

It didn't answer her, so she eased herself forward, pushing her hands off the floor and then her knees. She'd been taught to sit and stand and move properly, like a lady, but that didn't concern her now. She stood up in as unladylike a manner as she'd been sitting, slow, sluggish, and sprawling.

She stretching her arms above her head, the book still clasped in her hand. It was heavy, so she lowered it, glancing at the cover one more time before tossing it back into the box. It bounced a fraction up, then down, resting askew, but closed. With a push of her foot, the box slid back into its place at the rear of the closet.

She closed the door, went into the living room, and found one of her magazines in the neat stack on the coffee table. "How to Be Housewife of the Year" was the biggest headline, right beside another smiling woman. This woman, though, had a white apron in place of a white hat.

The magazine also promised tips for "New Knitting Patterns", "Money-Saving Tips on Groceries", and "Sun-Weather Fashion".

Sharon flipped to the recipe section.

*   *   *

The knock at the door came sometime between reading about checkered patterns and tunic tops. She jumped in the chair, startled, and the magazine flipped shut.

Her hopes for distraction had worked, it seemed.

Another knock, and Sharon pushed herself out of the chair, set the magazine on the top of the stack on the coffee table, and pressed her skirt down. As she walked to the door, she smoothed her hair back, throwing a quick glance at her reflection in the mirror next to the door before pasting a smile on her face, turning the handle, and inching the door open.

"Hello, ma'am." The man at the door was tall, with an easy smile, and he tipped his hat with a small dip of his head.

The briefcase at his feet gave him away. A salesman.

"Hello." She shook his extended hand.

Dark hair curled around his ears, but he'd brushed it back in a style reminiscent of Elvis.

Or James.

"Lovely day, isn't it?" His hand has still wrapped around hers. His grip was strong, firm, but not hard, and he shook hands as though his boss or manager had instructed him on the precise method of hand-shaking.

Salesmen and businessmen learn to shake hands. Nurses learn to make beds. Seems a lot of people are concerned with precision. Perhaps everyone is.

"Yes, it is."

He dropped her hand and flashed another smile. "Almost as lovely as yourself." Without missing a beat, he continued. "I know you're a busy woman. But if you give me a few minutes of your time, I can save you hours of work for months and years to come."

Months and years to come.

Sharon waited, knowing the request was coming. "I'm here today to talk to you about your kitchen. May I come in?"

Sharon stepped back and opened the door the rest of the way. "Of course," she said. She told her smile to broaden, and forced a levity and excitement to her voice. "I'd *love* to talk about my kitchen."

He stepped in, taking off his hat and bending as he crossed the threshold. He was tall enough he'd no doubt knocked himself on the head a few times in the past going in and out of homes. In fact, though she'd never measured, she was fairly certain this front entry was the largest doorway in her home, and he barely made it through that.

They stood in the entryway.

He towered over her. She'd always appreciated tall men.

"May I see the appliances in your kitchen, ma'am?"

"Of course."

If Albert had his study, the closest room to being "hers" was the kitchen. Few people set foot in the study, though, while few people stayed out of the kitchen. Albert's domain was closed off, private; Sharon's was the center of everything that went on in their home.

The salesman followed her down the hall. They paused at the living room, Sharon remembering the bar cart and her manners. "Would you like a drink, Mr…?"

"Please, call me William, ma'am. While a drink would surely hit the spot, just now I'm working, so I think just some iced tea or something would be fine, if that's alright with you."

"Perfectly."

She stepped through the doorway to the kitchen, forgetting about her ponderings about doorways and heights from a few minutes before, until she heard the thump and exclamation behind her.

"Shit," the salesman groaned, his hand pressed against his forehead, tilting forward, his other hand steadying against the offending door.

Sharon wasn't aware of gasping, but she heard the sharp intake and knew it came from her.

"I am so sorry," she said, taking a step back.

She could count on her fingers the number of times she'd heard someone swear in front of her, and was pretty sure most of those times had been Melinda.

The salesman - William - shook his head as though shaking the pain away. He winced at the movement. "Ow." He breathed deep. Sharon watched the slow rise and fall of his chest, visible still beneath his doubled-over frame.

"So sorry," she repeated.

"Not your fault," he said. "No need to apologize. In fact..." he trailed off, wincing again as he straightened, pressing a hand to the red mark forming just below where his hairline. There was a sharp hissing sound from between his teeth. He paused a moment, then tried again. "In fact, it is I who need to apologize to you, ma'am." He tilted his head in her direction, his hand still pressed to his forehead, and cleared his throat. "I'm afraid I used some very unseemly language just now. That was terribly ungentlemanly of me. My mother would have my hide if she knew I spoke like that in front of a lady, let alone one I didn't know. And in her own home, no less." He shook his head and flinched with the movement.

"I'm sure your mother would understand. Circumstances and all that." She stepped away from the kitchen table, waving her hand toward the vacant chair that held her husband's frame every morning and every evening. "Why don't you sit down? I can get you some ice."

He went to the table. As he sat, she busied herself finding the ice and wrapping it in a towel.

"Thank you," he said. "But if you knew my mother, she certainly would not understand. 'Excuses, excuses,' she'd say."

Sharon laughed at his high-pitched, nasally impression. He even wagged his index finger on his free hand for emphasis.

"In fact, Mother insists that proper behavior is even more important when caught off-guard."

"And injured?"

"Especially when injured. It shows our true colors, she says. It's all well and fine to be good and do what you ought when everything is going the way it's supposed to. But when you're caught off-guard, or injured, that's when it counts. That's when you show that you're a real gentleman. At your core, my mother would say."

She handed him the towel. When he cupped his hand beneath it, supporting the gathered ice, his hand brushed against hers. She pulled away as through his touch was a hot element on the stove, and went back to the refrigerator to get the iced tea he requested.

She hadn't touched the skin – any skin – of any other man but her husband, not since her father raised her veil and kissed her cheek before lowering it again at the end of the aisle. In fact, other than the patients at the hospital, she couldn't remember touching anyone other than Albert, regardless of gender, since her marriage.

Had she even shaken another hand?

The skin of her hand burned at the thought. She wondered, if she looked at it, would it be red? Would it be imprinted, etched? Would it match the mark on his forehead?

"You won't tell my mother on me, will you?"

"What?"

"For being so uncouth."

She could hear the smile behind the syllables, the teasing behind the words. She kept her back to him, pausing only the duration of an intake of breath before opening the fridge door.

"Of course not."

She closed the door, the pitcher of iced tea in her hand. She moved to the cupboard door and pulled out a glass. She thought the blue and orange flowers were cheerful when she first saw them in the store. They'd reminded her of sunshine and fields. Today, though, they didn't make her smile.

She poured the iced tea and straightened her shoulders. She turned, willing herself not to stare as she stepped toward the man sitting in her husband's place at their kitchen table. At last she raised her eyes to his.

He smiled at her, again. He was always smiling, it seemed.

He had a nice smile. His hair was like James', but his smile was warmer, less self-assured. His boss probably instructed him on how to smile in such a genuine way.

She held out the glass, and he tipped his head at it, still smiling. When he took it from her, their hands touched again.

She flinched away again. It wasn't him, she knew that. It wasn't actually his touch that reminded her of a thousand bee stings. It was someone else, a man no less, here in her domain. It was the fact that she hadn't touched another human being in eleven months.

It was his hair. James' hair, that had strolled into her dream and lodged itself in her rememberings and her day and the ticking of the clock bringing her closer and closer to her husband and the conversation she'd have with him.

She ran her thumb over the pads of her fingers where they'd brushed his. *Stop it,* she chastised herself. *Stop it. Stop it. Stop it.*

Her cheeks warmed, and she backed toward the sink, away from him, away from his Elvis-hair and his smile and away from his fingers, now wrapped around the glass, the orange and blue flowers peeking through.

He lifted the glass and took a sip. "This is very enjoyable, ma'am." Another sip. "Most refreshing."

She felt the cool metal of the sink through the material of her dress. *Stop it. Stop it. Stop it. You can't control a dream. It doesn't mean anything. You're going to tell him... tell him the parts you can, anyway. This man isn't James. The universe isn't tormenting you. Stop it.*

"What is it..." Something stopped the words from coming out, constricting her chest and her voice. She cleared her throat and tried again. "What is it you wanted to see in the kitchen - in my kitchen?"

He took another drink, still smiling, still holding the ice in his other hand.

The ice cubes clinked against the blue and orange flowers.

Why is it so warm in here?

He set the glass down and turned his attention to the case he carried. The fasteners clicked open, and Sharon wondered why the click of metal on metal seemed so loud. And the ticking of the clock - she'd never noticed it before - that hung on the far wall also was so loud it echoed.

She wanted to apologize, but she wasn't sure for what, so she bit her lip instead, saying nothing.

He didn't seem to notice. Instead, he launched into his recitation, all about the wonders of the new ovens that were on the market. "Glamour for your kitchen," he said, holding up an picture of a copper built-in. "Easy to clean," he continued, pointing at the image, as though his index finger on an advertisement proved anything about ease of scrubbing and polishing. As though he had any notion of how to actually clean an oven.

"An electric stove," he continued, holding up another photo. "So easy. Pushing a button, that's all it takes. So modern. The very latest in modern developments."

Sharon waved her hand toward her oven, sitting against the wall. Not built into the counter. Knobs instead of buttons. The metal bars gleamed from the polishing Sharon had done just the day previous. It was white, not copper. White.

White. Snow and innocence and the pearls she wore at her wedding.

"I don't think my husband would like me ordering a new oven or stove."

"Oh, he would be so happy to have such wonderful meals prepared for him. I imagine any man coming home to such a lovely wife would be happy. And with these newest conveniences in kitchens, you would have more time available. Less time cleaning, less time prepping, less time cooking. More time with him. So every day he could look forward to an easy, delicious meal, and the prospect of actually spending some time with his lovely wife."

Sharon shook her head again and twisted her fingers together. "It would be too expensive. I don't think he would give me the money for something so... so grand."

The salesman kept smiling, setting down the glossy photos and picking up a different catalogue.

"Perhaps something simpler then? Surely your husband would give you the money for a bit of modern flair, a bit of glamour. Treat yourself with these new cannisters" - a set of six yellow plastic ones - "or this. A nonstick pan. Everyone had to have one. Light. Cooks evenly."

As if he knew anything about cooking evenly. As if he'd ever cooked anything.

Sharon bit her lip again, watching the way his eyes crinkled at the corners.

"It's just what every modern housewife could wish for."

Something flared within her then, some ember of frustration that she knew wasn't supposed to be there. Her palms felt damp. She smoothed them across the front of her dress. The dress that matched her neighbor's house.

Just what every modern housewife could wish for. Surely she should wish for it? Surely she should dream of a copper oven, a built-in electric range. Buttons. Plastic. More time with her husband. Delicious meals waiting for him. Yellow cannisters. A nonstick pan.

Just what she should wish for.

She remembered the determination from the morning, leaning at the sink, so close to how she was standing now.

How much of my life will be spent at this sink?

She had vowed to be a good housewife, to not think of James. Think only of meals and laundry and cleaning.

Maybe it was better yet to not think about anything.

"Perhaps," she nodded at the catalogue. "Perhaps the pan? Or maybe…" she glanced around, at the white oven, the counters. "Maybe something like a new teapot?" She imagined neighborhood ladies coming over for tea. Imagined herself drinking tea in the afternoons instead of whiskey.

"Just the thing!" He flipped a couple of pages, and held up another glossy image. "This one, with the flowers." It was yellow, with orange flowers that almost, but not quite, matched the ones on the glass sitting near him, ice beginning to melt.

"Sure. That one. Perfect."

"And the pan?"

"And the pan." She smiled. *Look excited. Look like this is just what you want. Your day is complete now. Your week. You get to treat yourself. What more could you want?*

"Excellent. You will be so happy."

"Yes." Her lips twitched, her head bobbed up once, then down. "So happy."

CHAPTER 11

3:00 pm

The salesman was gone by the time Bonnie arrived. Her hat was barely off, her matching handbag barely set down, before she began regaling Sharon with the latest news in her children's lives.

"Matthew is down. Went right out. He's been doing that lately; down and out like a light, you know. And Julie, Julie is just so helpful. She's colouring now, you know. Every day she draws another picture for me, for her father, for her brother. Such a little mother." Bonnie set her hat, a dark blue with a flower, on the side table.

"They're okay on their own?" Sharon watched her run a hand over her hair, smoothing back the frayed ends.

"Oh, of course. Like I said, Matthew's down. And Julie is there, and knows where I am. She has strict instructions to come get me the moment Matthew wakes up."

"She certainly sounds capable."

"Of course. Like I said, such a little mother. Besides," she raised her eyebrow, raised a shoulder, dropped both, "I'm only down the street."

Sharon led Bonnie into the kitchen and grabbed the glass from the table where the salesman had left it.

"Have company before I got here?" Bonnie settled herself at the table while Sharon set the glass in the sink and started heating the kettle for tea. She thought of the new teapot she'd just ordered. *Just what every modern housewife could wish for.*

"Just a salesman," Sharon said, taking down one of her Tupperware containers full of tea. She measured out the leaves, wondering about the hippies she'd read of earlier. They drank tea, she knew from reading some other earlier article, but discussed things like consciousness and awakenings. Or maybe the tea was supposed to encourage that? She wondered what type of tea affected those things. She wondered if she'd try it, if given the chance. She wondered if she'd ever be given the chance.

She seemed to be wondering a lot today.

"That dreamy one?"

Sharon paused only a moment, her hand hovering over the pale green seal before snapping it back onto the container, pushing down in the centre to exhaust the air. "What do you mean?" She hoped her voice was light, nonchalant, indifference skipping over the words like a pebble over water, rather than tripping over them, plunking and sinking in meaning and tone.

"Oh you know. Tall. Dark. Handsome. The whole package, you know. Really tall. Peddlin' kitchenwares and uuoh, That one."

"Oh. Yeah, I guess that's him. He tried to sell me a new oven and stove."

"Tried to? Honey, if he'd have asked, I'd have bought everything that man wanted me to."

Sharon tapped her fingers on the countertop, twice, then turned to face her friend. And Bonnie was indeed her friend, or at least one of the closest things she had to a friend here. Shortly after they'd moved in, just after the wedding, Sharon opened the door to Bonnie standing on their front step, holding an infant in a yellow blanket, a girl with dark curls and a pink bow standing beside her. The child had a casserole in her tiny hands, held up, an offering to housewifery and new neighbor propriety.

Since then, the older woman - not much older, Sharon guessed, though she never thought to ask - walked the few steps from her house to Sharon's every couple days, leaving the little child in charge for an hour or so while the baby napped. She spoke of almost nothing except her children, while Sharon crossed her ankles, nodded, offered refreshments, sipped at her tea.

Sharon was thankful for the visits, for the company, for the facade of friendship.

She never returned the trip though, never made her own trek from door to door. Bonnie never invited her, and Sharon never thought to ask.

"So what'd you buy?" Bonnie asked. "The whole shebang?"

"Nah. A new pan, one of those non-stick ones. And a new teapot. Pretty."

"That's lovely, sweetie. What else?"

"Nothing."

"Nothing? Really? From that dreamboat?"

"Bonnie, no one says dreamboat anymore."

Bonnie waved her hand in front of her as though Sharon's reprimand was an annoying mosquito.

"Don't be such a goose. I'd have gone through every catalogue that man had, twice. Asked him all kinds of questions, too, just so's I could have him around. Look at him a bit, talk to him a bit, you know."

"I wouldn't want to waste his time like that. And besides, Albert…"

"Oh honey, nothing wrong with looking. Just 'cause you're married don't mean you can't cast an eyeball 'round once in a while. You don't think Albert ever looks at the secretaries and operators at his office?"

Sharon rubbed her fingertip over her bottom lip. She hadn't really thought of it before, but admitting that, even to herself, sounded foolish. "Of course. Of course he does, it's just, that's different."

"'Course it's different. Don't mean it's any less true."

Sharon looked down, shrugged. *Does it bother me that Albert looks at other women? Finds other women attractive?* She didn't know.

It bothered her that she didn't know.

"So what did he show you? What's the word in kitchen appliances these days? You know Ruth Miller, she redid her whole kitchen, all in blue. Her oven is right in the wall now. That's all copper. Looks great with the blue. So modern."

Just what every modern housewife could wish for.

"Yes, he showed me one of those built-in copper ones. A picture of one, I mean."

"I tell you, that's so fancy. Just kills me. I'd probably have said yes, someone like him offering me something like that."

Sharon shrugged, turned back to the kettle, which had started to whistle. While she fixed the tea, she heard the click of Bonnie's heels moving away from her, then the clinking of glass on glass.

"Course was probably super costly, wasn't it? Redoin' the whole thing. Ruth got the money, course, what with her hubby and that new promotion and all. I keep sayin', once she pops out a coupla babies she can kiss some of that cheddar bye-bye, but for now she might as well spend the money and enjoy it. Besides, nice to have it done now so when those little ones come it's all set and ready to go."

Sharon let Bonnie's chattering roll over her. Only the kettle and the cups concerned her.

Soon enough Bonnie was beside her again, whiskey decanter in hand. "Let's fix up that tea proper."

Sharon laughed, sharp and loud enough to startle her. She clamped her teeth shut, stoppering the sound.

Bonnie didn't seem to notice. Instead, she sloshed a generous dollop of whiskey into each cup. Sharon topped up each with the tea she'd been steeping.

"Let's drink these outside." Bonnie picked up the cup nearest her. "Sound a plan?"

"Sure." Sharon followed her out the door, then around the side to the back of the house, to the concrete patio. Bonnie settled herself into the nearest of two chairs.

Sharon sat as well, aware that she was now directly in front of the house that matched her dress. Maybe if Bonnie looked at her, she would blend right in, camouflaged, hidden, a part of the background.

She drank a mouthful of tea. It was too hot, the whiskey too strong. She swallowed it anyway. Ignoring the burning, blinking back the tears that formed as the liquid slid down her throat, she let her eyes search the backyard. Just lawn, grass that Albert cut almost every Sunday. She tried to imagine a swing set in the corner, toys scattered around, but the picture escaped her.

She sighed, took another drink, and realized that Bonnie was talking.

"'Course, Julie wasn't really reading, but it was so cute to see her flipping those pages, you know, telling Matthew the little story. She'd just read that one so many times, it's her favourite, you know, and she was pointing to the pictures. Just the sweetest thing. She's a natural mother, that one. Always following after me. Been thinking about getting her one of them plastic vacuum cleaners, you know the ones? Maybe even a kitchen set. They come in pink. Just the sweetest thing. Teaches them, too, you know."

"Sure."

Bonnie raised the cup to her lips. She didn't so much as blink as she swallowed, though Sharon knew Bonnie had an equal level of whiskey in her own teacup. Bonnie lowered her teacup, and Sharon again turned to consider the corner.

Maybe a garden.

Sharon remembered that her mother had had a garden. Her grandmother, too. When she was a kid she'd follow after them. Her mom even had special shoes just for the garden, brown ones, the lowest heels she had, all worn and soft and dirty. She had a big basket that stayed by the back door, and when Sharon was little she was allowed to tag along after her, carrying the basket full of the carrots and onions and turnips they pulled from the earth.

Was she allowed to carry it, or was she supposed to? Was she being taught, the same way Bonnie wanted little Julie to be *laughing. This is food, this is how you feed your husband, your family. This is your job.*

"Bonnie?"

"Hmm?"

Sharon sipped, blinked back more tears. She wanted the drink to take off the edge, thankful for the heat and the whiskey for an excuse for her discomfort, for any words that fell out of her mouth wrong.

"I was thinking..." She weighed the phrasing, measured her tone. "That is, I was wondering... Julie and Matthew..."

"Yeah?"

"You love them, right? I mean, of course you do."

"'Course I do."

Sharon could feel Bonnie's gaze on her, could see that upturned eyebrow in her peripheral vision. She kept her eyes forward, though, on the corner of the yard where she imagined - where she should have imagined - a swing set.

"It's just, did you always want them? Kids, I mean. Did you always, I don't know... Did you always know you'd have children? Boys and girls in your house, in your backyard?"

"Something wrong, sweetie? That's a funny thing to wonder."

"I know." Sharon looked at her tea and coughed. She tried a small smile. "Must just be the whiskey, making me wonder."

Bonnie chuckled, leaned over, and clinked her teacup against Sharon's. "Cheers to that, then!" Another drink.

Sharon looked at her, attempted smile still on her lips. She dropped it as she diverted her eyes.

"Well, since you asked, yes, I did know I'd have kids. I hoped for a boy and a girl, and I got one of each. Of course every woman wants that, one of each, I mean. Course not all get as lucky as me. Poor Alice down two houses? Four boys. God, can you imagine? What a mess to pick up after them all. So dirty, you know, always trackin' in dirt and jazz. Is that what's bothering you?"

"I don't know."

It wasn't, though.

"Tell you the truth though, I got mighty scared about it when we first, well, after we first got married, you know. Scared of being a grown up. Scared I'd be a real bad mom or something. But it's working out so far. 'Course we women are built for it, designed for it, you know. We figure it all out right quick." Another drink. "Another thing, something I haven't told you before, I'm thinking another one would be real nice. Babies are so swell, you know."

"Yeah." Sharon, too, took another drink. She only blinked once this time.

"Their little hands and little toes. And they smell good. All soft and sweet. Even don't mind their crying. Not usually, anyway. Sure sometimes in the middle of the night it gets a little tiresome, but they're pretty nice. You'll learn one day soon enough, sure enough."

"Right." The words poked holes in Sharon, and she felt her blood drain away. She bit her lip.

"Why you wonderin' so much, honey? You writin' a book?"

Sharon laughed again, that same too sharp, too loud laugh, but this time she let the sound echo across her lawn and against her fence, against the green house next door, against the empty corner where a swingset should sit. It assaulted the tree, harsh, cutting.

She didn't know why she laughed.

Bonnie chuckled, quieted, stared at her. Sharon knew she should stop the rise and fall, the bursts of her laughter. She gulped, her guffaws turning to giggles, then aloud, sounding, almost hiccupping blasts, then nothing.

The effort left her breathing heavy and deep. Sharon sighed, bringing herself under control. Tears still clung to her eyes, and she wasn't sure whether they were from the laughter at a comment that wasn't funny, or the whiskey sloshing in her teacup, or all those other things she was holding down within herself. She wasn't sure what the difference was between all those things, if there even was a difference. And she wasn't sure if she wanted to know.

She wasn't sure of much.

The quiet that followed was more pronounced because of the outburst from a moment before. The women drank their tea in short sips, silent, waiting.

"Sorry," she said, still staring ahead, hesitant to even blink.

"For what? For acting a little crazy?"

"Yeah."

"No sweat, sweetie. Just the other day, Julie started giggling at something. It went on way too long, you know how it is, and then she was hiccupping and sniffling and just couldn't stop. I asked her about it later, of course, and she said she was laughing, then laughing at herself for laughing so much 'cause she sounded so funny. Ain't that just the thing? So smart for a little ankle-biter, isn't she?"

"So smart."

"That's what happened just now, isn't it? You got laughing and couldn't stop laughing?"

"Yeah. Definitely. That's what happened."

"Of course it is. You're not crazy at all, sweetie. Stuff like that, well, it just happens all the time, you know. Sometimes I get so, well, just so... Anyway, it doesn't matter. Just sometimes I get a little crazy. Laughing or... or whatever. It doesn't mean anything."

"It doesn't?"

"Of course not."

"Thanks, Bonnie." Sharon drained the rest of her tea in a single gulp. Even more of the whiskey had settled at the bottom.

She sputtered, and her tears gathered in number and strength. "Hey, can I ask you one more thing?"

"I s'pose so."

Sharon finally looked at her friend, really looked at her, for the first time since they sat down. "Do you have a swing set at your house?"

Bonnie tilted her head, glaced at Sharon, looked down, then back up. "Sure do, sweetie. How come? You… uh… you in need of one?" Again her eyes moved down, then back up, seeming to search Sharon.

"Oh. No." Realization struck, and Sharon shook her head, too fast, too hard. Her tears blurred her vision. "No, nothing like that. No. It's just, I was wondering. No. Just, this backyard. It seems… um, it seems empty. Was just…"

"Wondering?" Bonnie offered.

"Yeah. I suppose so." Sharon sighed. "Wondering."

Bonnie nodded, shifted her posture so she, too faced the lawn. It was a little patchy in the one corner, the one Sharon had been staring at before.

"Yeah. We got a swing set. Just the thing, you know, for Julie. And then Matthew, when he gets big enough. And then if we did end up with another little one, all the better. Handy, you know. I don't have to take time to walk them to the playground. Julie can just go play in the backyard, and there's the set, right there, while I'm working on dinner or whatever. Can see it right out the window." Bonnie nodded at the corner. "When you need one, honey, that spot right there would be just perfect. In the corner. That's where you put it."

"Yeah?"

"Oh sure." Bonnie tipped her cup back, finishing her own drink. "I can imagine it perfectly."

CHAPTER 12

4:00 pm

Bonnie left for home before little Julie came to find her, so Sharon didn't get to see the little pigtailed girl. Julie was adorable, after all. Matthew too. With their cherubic blue eyes and chubby cheeks, they both looked like they belonged on greeting cards, those Christmas ones with sparkles around the edges and on the ornaments on tree. No one could argue that little kids like that were not cute.

Unless you were one of those kid-hating women Sharon's father talked about.

She wasn't one of them. She did like kids. She thought Julie was cute, that Matthew was cute. And when she held little Matthew, or when Julie told her she was pretty, she did feel that twinge, somewhere in her sinew, that pulled her to them. That feeling, that twinge, was so similar to the one she used to feel when she carried Molly around as a kid herself, not any bigger than Julie. Was it the same feeling, perhaps? Or had it morphed, altered, changed as a reflection in a dirty mirror? There, almost, but not quite, her?

And why did she accept the twinge in reference to nursing, but likened it to a dirty reflection in reference to motherhood?

After Bonnie left, Sharon paused to adjust the chairs they'd been sitting in. She straightened each one to the left, then the right, then the left just the smallest nudge again when she overcorrected them. She gathered their teacups and went inside, through the backdoor this time, reminding herself again of the tiny tear in the screen and to add it to the mental list of things to ask Albert for.

Her mother would have had a conniption fit had she known company was over while clothing was out on the line.

She set the teacups beside the sink once she was inside. Beside, of course, never in, so as not to chip the edges. Then she scooped up the laundry basket and headed back out.

The bird that flitted among the tree branches and through her mind earlier was nowhere to be seen. Sharon hoped it flew away. Long gone, soaring off to see new places. What landscapes would change beneath its wings? What cities and towns and farms and rivers and lakes would that little bird see that she never would?

Maybe she'd scared it off during her recent hysterics.

She pulled off each item from the line, dropping the clothespins back into their bag with a click. Each item was snapped into the air, shaken once, then folded, seam to seam, corner to corner, before it was at last draped in the basket. Snap. Shake. Fold. Set. Repeat.

When Sharon hefted the basket, now full, back to her hip, she stood, staring at the corner Bonnie had suggested would make the perfect spot for a swing set. She squinted her left eye, then her right, trying to imagine it. She shook her head. Maybe a little garden, but not a swing set.

She shifted her focus to the tree, to the branches and leaves that rustled now. She hadn't noticed when the wind died down, but it was calm now. Now there was only light rustling, the sound of pieces of paper being crinkled, balled up before being tossed in a wastebasket, the sound of baseball cards in the spokes of a bicycle's wheel just before the rider picks up speed.

But there was no bird.

She readjusted the basket, tightened her grip, and turned her back to the tree, to the branch the now-empty branch. She went inside, letting the screen door bang shut behind her.

*   *   *

Once the laundry was put away, the teacups washed and dried and put back in the cabinet, the counters wiped down, Sharon leaned her back against the sink, waiting.

Waiting for what, she wasn't sure.

She shifted her gaze from the clock on the wall to the fridge to the cupboards, then back to the clock. White framed in yellow, plastic, another wedding gift.

"Just one more hour," she told the second hand, making its slow pilgrimage past each of its numbers. Going, going, only to end up right back where it started.

"One more hour, and Albert will be home."

The meat was still thawing. She would peel the potatoes in another half hour. Even after only a single year, the timing of this song and dance was down to clockwork. Each step, each tick and each tock measured out in perfect timing. Moving around the tasks, the hours in the day, only to end up right back where she started.

She took pride in her abilities, in understanding her mother's teachings in how to keep a home. Still, she wondered at herself for that sense of pride. What purpose did it serve? Did it matter if everything was timed perfectly? And if she was so good at this already, then what? What change stretched out in front of her? How could she improve in another year? Five years? Ten? Twenty?

Fifty?

Was that all that was ahead of her now? New recipes, more efficient house cleaning, meals prepared to the perfect second?

She leaned back even further, allowing her back to curve against the edge of the counter. She wondered how far back she could lean before the counter would start biting into her skin through her dress.

She remembered how James once dipped her back to kiss her, bending her at the end of a dance, almost as far as she was bent back now. His arm had snaked around her back, in almost the same place as the edge of the laminate now.

James.

She pursed her lips and emptied her lungs. Pushing out her breath, pushing away from the countertop, she also pushed away the memories, the unwelcome thoughts. She stumbled a step, but caught herself.

This wouldn't do. She couldn't just sit around and wait until the appropriate time to start the appropriate dinner for her appropriate husband and their appropriate life.

She needed something. Something that stepped out of place, stepped out of all the appropriateness.

Just a small stumble, just a small step.

⼁   ⼂   ⼂

Melinda answered on the third ring.

"It's Sharon."

"How the hell are ya?"

Sharon smiled, which of course Melinda couldn't see. Her cousin was still the only woman she knew who didn't sound ridiculous cursing.

"Oh, I'm good. Just calling to say hi."

"Swell, but not buyin' that."

"You're not?"

"Nope. You never call just to say hi. Oh, you always say that's why you're callin', but there's always more to the story, ya know. Some ulterior motive."

"Is there?"

"Mmhmm. Only you're always too damned polite to let on, so we get to do the whole song and dance around the small talk part for a while, and the whole time I'm tryin' to figure out just what it is, but I never do, ya know, and then you say somethin' that tips me off, and then finally I figure it out."

"This is all news to me, Melinda."

"Course it is. That's 'cause even after I figure out what's wrong with you, I can't let on, ya know. 'Cause what would I say? So I don't, and instead we gossip about the family and such and so on."

Sharon peeled up the corner of the top page from the paper pad she kept by the phone. It was white — *snow and innocence and the pearls I wore to my wedding* — with the words "message for" printed at the top. The words were in yellow.

Why is there so much yellow in my kitchen? Sharon blinked at the clock, then again at the paper pad. *I don't even like yellow all that much.*

"So why don't we just save some time and you just come on out with it now?" Melinda's voice was light, but not breathy, like stones skipping across a lake. Or perhaps her voice was more like the lake. There was more you couldn't see; Sharon was confident anyone would recognize that. But it was a voice that didn't take itself too seriously.

Sharon had heard herself in a voice recording once, one of those tape recorders they used in dictation in her typing classes. They had to learn to use the machine, and as part of the demonstration all the ladies had lined up and practiced. Sharon's voice was like everything else about her. It took itself so seriously it could sign up for a mortgage and dispense wisdom. If Melinda's voice was stones skipping across a lake, Sharon thought hers was more like an anchor sinking to the bottom.

"I have no idea what you're talking about," she said, trying to bring that anchor voice at least a little closer to the surface.

"Oh, sure. And you just got all high-pitched now for no reason, right?"

"I didn't get all high-pitched."

"Yeah you did. It's all fine, though. Groovy, 'kay? Just thought I'd save you some time and be upfront and just ask what's wrong. Somethin's always wrong. But I knew you couldn't answer."

"What do you mean? How did you know that?"

"Share-Bear. You couldn't answer what's wrong because you don't know. You know somethin's wrong, else-wise you wouldn't be callin', but you don't really know what it is exactly. Can't put your finger on it, can ya?"

She could put her finger on it, though. The appointment yesterday that led to the dream last night that led to the memories berating her all day. But all of that choked her, was a stopper in her throat, and she couldn't talk about it.

"Melinda, I don't know what you're talking about."

" 'Course you do. You're just too damn polite to say anything, or to answer, or even to admit somethin's wrong because god knows nothin's s'posed to be wrong."

"Melinda…"

The pause stretched out in front of her. When she looked down, Sharon's lips pressed into a thin line. She stilled her hands over the top piece of paper, all torn up, with only the "mes" from "message for" still in place in the top corner. *Mes. Mess. It's a mess alright,* she thought.

"Look, Sharon. Share-Bear. I'm sorry. That was a shit way to answer the phone. Just bombard ya like that."

"It's okay."

"Nope. Nope it's not. I don't know what I was thinkin'."

Sharon said nothing, just waited. She knew Melinda, knew she sometimes morphed into a train speeding ahead, regardless of where the track was headed or who was tied to it.

Melinda's sigh crackled with static through the phone. "Can we, like, start this whole conversation over again?"

Sharon smiled. "No reason to do that. No damage done."

"I just get a little wacko sometimes."

"I know. It's okay."

There was another pause. Sharon drummed her fingers against the scraps of paper, avoiding the half-word "mes" and resisting the urge to tear that up as well.

"So… so what did you want to talk to me about? Why did you call me before I went all wacko on you?"

"You aren't that bad, Melinda. Like I said, I was just calling to say hi."

"Uh huh."

"Honestly." Sharon averted her eyes to the ceiling. She added "dust the lightbulbs" to her mental to-do list. "I guess… I suppose I just wanted to hear your voice. See how you are."

"Oh. Well, that's sweet, Share-Bear. I'm doin' swell, you know. As always." A pause. "Um… how about you?"

"Just swell, too."

"Yeah?"

"Yeah." Sharon hadn't meant her answer to be so quick, so sharp, so clipped. But she had, and the word hung in the air around her, a staccato period punctuating itself through the telephone cord. She was sure Melinda would comment on that. Of course she would.

"Uh huh." Another pause. Sharon imagined Melinda weighing each word, showing surprising restraint, looking both directions before plunging her train ahead.

But Melinda surprised her. "Well that's just… swell," was all she said. She changed her tone and the subject then. "So what did you do today, Share-Bear? You weren't all by yourself in that house all day, were you?"

"Oh no." *Thank god.* "I went to the hospital. Read a book to some kids."

"How was that?" Another tone change. Melinda's voice dropped, her train screeching to a stop, concern dripping from her syllables. "You okay?"

"Oh yeah." Sharon ignored the mental image of the memory of her gasping, screwing her eyes shut tight, fighting tears and bile and everything else wanting to escape her. "Just fine. That was… Well I mean…." *Why am I lying to Melinda, of all people? She knows. She understands. As much as anyone can, anyway.* "It isn't easy, sometimes. Sometimes it gets to me. Today was mostly okay. But there was a moment… But it was mostly okay."

"Don't know how you can do that. I don't even like kids and seeing them in hospitals. Hell that'd be hard on anyone. And with everything you've been through… Well, don't know how you can put yourself through that all the time."

"Everything I've been through?"

"You know what I mean, Share-Bear."

"Yeah, but you're talking like I survived some horrible disease or something."

"You kind of did. You could have died, you know. And that fever…. You don't remember how bad it was, how long you were just on that bed. When you weren't passed right out you'd cry or yell… I should've taken you to the hospital. If something'd happened to you I'd never forgive myself."

"I remember enough. You did want to take me to the hospital. I wouldn't let you."

"You screamed and cried more if I even said the word *hospital* or *doctor*. Screw that, though. I should've anyway. It's not like you were in any position to stop me."

"You know you couldn't have done that. Any doctor would have figured out why I was sick. And then… Well, who knows what would have happened. It's illegal, Melinda. Or at least it was then. Now…"

"Oh I read the news. Still not like you can just up and go get one. Girls still gettin' sick, still dyin' from it. Might not be illegal like it used to be, but still not really legal either, ya know? And them girls in the States, they all have to go 'bout it illegally, or else come up here."

"I know. Believe me, I know."

"But still, just doesn't seem right I didn't even take you to the doctor. Now maybe I could've."

"It doesn't matter. That was then. You couldn't take me to the hospital."

"Probably just would've gotten a fine any which way."

"Or jail time. And even if it was just a fine, did you have the money to pay that fine? Because I spent all mine on having… on getting… I mean the doctor… well…"

"I know."

Sharon thanked Melinda in her mind for saving her from having to say the words. She couldn't; she hadn't been able to admit it, even to herself, since the day she woke up from that delirium, that fever.

"So that would have been jail time anyway."

"Jail is better than dead, Share-Bear. You could've died. I was worried you were goin' to. Looked pretty close a few times."

"You said that, yeah. But I ended up okay. Everything ended up fine. I didn't die. And I didn't end up broke or in jail either. So it turned out to be a good thing you didn't take me to the hospital."

"That's just luck. If you'd've died… or ended up permanently sick or somethin'…. That'd be on me, you know. For not steppin' in. For not gettin' you help, not takin' you to the hospital."

"You only helped me, Melinda. You didn't do anything wrong. You weren't the one who…" Sharon trailed off. She couldn't say the words, but she knew where all the blame lay, and none of it was with her cousin. She cleared her throat, tried again. "It was the doctor who… well, maybe he made a mistake somehow. You hear stories, you know, about dirty instruments, conditions that aren't great, doctors who don't do it right."

"Of course. They know they won't get caught. Especially then, before the law changed. Or I mean, kinda changed."

"Bill C-150." Sharon closed her eyes and remembered the paper under her fingertips the morning she read the news. It was legal. Under very specific conditions, yes, but still legal.

"Sure. But like you said, that was then. They knew you couldn't go to the fuzz. So why would they worry? Why take the time and effort? He already had your money. And way too much money, if you ask me. Bastards can charge whatever they want. They know they can get away with it."

"Yeah."

"And if someone gets sick or dies, what do they care?"

"I'm sure it wasn't intentional, if that was even what happened." Sharon drummed her fingers again. "And it's not like it would only be the doctor's fault. It was what it was. Is what it is. Things happen. If I hadn't... If James and I hadn't..."

"Oh give it up, Share-Bear. What a crock. It happened. You just said it: It is what it is. You aren't a nun. What else could you do? Him leavin' you like that. He shouldn't've cheated. He shouldn't've run away."

"No." She remembered the tail-lights. "No, he shouldn't have. But he did. And that wasn't why I... made the choice I did."

"I know."

"What else could I have done?"

"That's right. What else were you goin' to do? Your parents, well, your dear ol' dad anyway, made it very clear what would happen if you ever found yourself in the family way. He'd've probably beaten it out of you."

Sharon screwed her eyes shut against memories of nightmares and blood and pain.

"That happens, you know," Melinda went on. "Girlfriend of mine, Lucy, happened to her. 'Cept it was her husband, not her daddy. Hits her and she starts to bleed and then there's a trip to the hospital and no more baby."

"That's awful."

"Hell yeah it is. And you think your dad wouldn't've lost it on you? He threatened to do it enough times. Or worse. He could've just beaten you and turned you out and then what?"

"Yeah."

"And how exactly would you take care of yourself, let alone someone else who cries all the time? You couldn't finish school like that, couldn't work. You couldn't buy groceries. And what if it got sick? Or you? Where would you live? How would you live?"

"I guess I could have... I don't know. Done something."

"Yeah. Live on the streets. Go find one of those communes maybe. Those hippie groups. I couldn't even have let you live with me. Though I'd've loved to. You know how my landlady gets."

"I know."

"You did what you had to."

"I know that. I really do. I knew it then. I know it now. That doesn't mean I have to like it."

"Solid. You're right. It doesn't. Just like it doesn't mean I had to listen to you when you refused to let me take you to the hospital. Just because it was the right thing to be doin' doesn't mean it was the right right thing, ya know?"

"Yeah, I know."

I could tell Melinda now. She knew about the... well, she knows about before. This was different. If she understood then, she'll understand now. Sharon's hand that was not holding the phone drifted down to rest on her belly. No, the words wouldn't come.

"Listen, I know we've been over this and over this and over this again. You listen to me now. It's awful. I wish you didn't have to.... Well, you didn't have to do what you did. But you didn't see any other way."

"Melinda ''

"Share-Bear. Maybe there was one. Another way. But maybe there wasn't. You did what you thought you had to, I wish you didn't have to, but I really wish you didn't have to make the decision in the first place. And I wish you didn't have to do it alone."

Sharon bit her lip, sighed. "You were there. I wasn't alone."

"I don't count.'

"You count the most."

"BS. What good did I do? Zilch, that's what."

"You were there."

There was quiet then, heavy and laden with gut-wrenching emotions and memories, of both things once said and things that could never be spoken.

"I mean…" Melinda cleared her throat. "Share-Bear, you should've had someone with you who could take care of you. Someone who'd take you to the hospital if you needed to go. Someone who didn't get scared. Someone who could pay for a fine or hell, even a better… procedure… in the first place."

"If I had that…" Sharon trailed off. She cleared her throat and tried again, her response little more than a breathy whisper, so quiet she wasn't sure Melinda could ever hear it on the other end of the line. "If I had that, I wouldn't have felt I needed to go and… do that… in the first place. I wouldn't have…" She cleared her throat again, and raised her eyes to the ceiling, blinking back hurt and tears and the past. "I wouldn't have even been in that situation."

Sharon swallowed and lowered her eyes. She tore up what was left of the top piece of paper. She wouldn't be telling Melinda, at least not now.

She looked at the "mes" in her hand, then tore that again. Little pieces of little scraps flittered around her like confetti for a birthday party that baby would never have.

Or like snow.

Snow. Innocence. The pearls I wore to my wedding.

She closed her eyes.

"Everything turned out fine, Melinda. Everything is okay. You were there. That's what I needed. I wasn't alone." She opened her eyes again, breathed in slow, then let it out even slower. "We don't even need to be talking about this anymore." *In. Out. In. Out.* The same way she'd breathed this morning, trying to calm her heart and mind after waking up from her unwelcome dream.

"We're just gonna take turns comfortin' each other, huh?"

"That's what we do, I suppose. But I'm okay. It was a lousy situation, but it is what it is. Was what it was. It's done, and everything is fine."

"Just swell, huh?"

"Yeah." Sharon swept the confetti paper into her hand. "Just swell."

CHAPTER 13

5:00 pm

The potatoes were peeled, quartered, and cooking away in their boiling water when Sharon heard the front door open and close. The sounds always startled her, something about the awareness of another human presence in her home, letting itself in of its own free will, interrupting her thoughts and silence and to-do lists.

Mixed vegetables, boiled, peas and carrots and corn. She stirred the medley as she heard Albert's steps in the porch. She knew those steps, knew from the rise and fall and pause that he was hanging up his hat.

How many years would it take for a path to be worn from his re-entrance every evening? Door to hat hook, hat hook to living room chair, living room chair to table, table back to chair, chair to bed. Throw in a trip to his study once in a while, just for variety.

And where would her path be worn down? Sink to oven to counter to table, she imagined. Where else could it be?

She checked the meatloaf, the potatoes, the vegetables. She brought out the bowl of buttered nuts she'd prepared, and headed to the living room. The bowl went on the coffee table by Albert's favourite chair.

He walked in the room, and she smiled at the way he nodded at her, the way he dipped his head and the grin on his face. He did like seeing her, she knew that, knew it in the way his eyes fixated on her as soon as he walked in the room after coming home from work. She remembered her mother talking about men at their work, how they get tired of being surrounded by only men every day, how they look forward to the tranquility and warmth of home, of the beauty of their wives, of a good meal.

Sharon pressed her lips together. She'd never thought to wonder how her mother, who hadn't worked outside of the home a single day of her life, knew about what men did and did not feel at work.

Her mother did know things, though. She knew about when to plant the tulips, when to harvest the herbs, how to stretch the laundry money and the groceries, how to mend and repurpose clothing so something decades old and worn looked new and modern.

And she knew about knights and princesses and happily ever afters, and how to smooth the wayward tendrils of her daughter's hair night after night

The brave knight coming home after a day of knighthood, coming home to the beautiful princess to made his drink and his supper. She blinked away the memory of her mother's hands as her own smoothed down her dress again.

Her smile back at Albert was genuine. He was happy to be home, happy to see her, and she was happy for that.

"Hello, darling," Albert said, stepping to her and bending to kiss her cheek.

"Hello. How was work?"

Albert sat in his favourite chair, settling in and stretching his arms in front of him. "Oh, fine. Fine."

He grabbed a handful of nuts and tossed them toward his mouth. One. Two. Three. They plopped into his gaping maw, one right after the other. Sharon narrowed her eyes as one missed and fell to the floor. Albert either didn't notice or didn't care. He didn't react at all, except to toss another one. Another miss. He caught the one after, though, and the one after that.

Sharon turned her back to him and the nuts discarded on her clean floor and instead busied herself at the bar cart. She poured Albert his drink, whiskey with soda, a much darker hue than the ones she'd drank earlier. Another drink for her, too, a Manhattan. She even dropped a Maraschino cherry into the glass from the jar under the cart, letting a bit of the amber splash up, but not enough to actually spill. There wasn't that much in her glass. She wasn't a lush, after all.

Albert wiped his hands against his pant legs before he reached for his drink. Sharon narrowed her eyes at his fingers, still glistening from the buttered topping to the nuts, but said nothing as he reached for the drink. There would be smudges along the glass now.

He took a healthy swallow, sighed, and leaned his head back. "That's it right there, darling."

"What is?" She sat on the couch adjacent to his chair, but didn't look at him. Instead, she tilted her drink to the left, then the right. The cherry dipped and bobbed, a tiny red iceberg in the ocean of amber.

"This moment, right here." His chair creaked, as it always did when he leaned back a certain way. "Coming home, to you, my darling. All day I just can't wait to get home and see you."

"Is that so?" Sharon still didn't pry her eyes away from the cherry. Maybe she had it wrong; maybe the cherry wasn't an iceberg; maybe it was a life preserver.

"Of course it is. I hate to leave here every day, this lovely home you've made. You're so lucky you don't have to."

She tilted the glass again. "Lucky," she echoed.

"But then I get to come home. To you. And I get to sit here with you. Just you and me, sitting here together. Just the two of us."

"Just the two of us?"

"For now, of course."

Sharon felt blood rush to her head and her temples pound. "What does that mean? *For now?*"

"Oh, you know. Eventually there will be more of us. We'll be a real family."

At last she pulled her eyes from her drink. "I thought we were a real family."

"Of course we are, darling. I just meant that one day we'll be a bigger family. And until then I so love coming home to you."

Don't, Sharon told herself. *Don't start an argument. He was being nice. He meant to be nice. Don't make it mean.* She inhaled, willed herself to refocus on the cherry and ignore his words and the implications she heard there. "That's nice," she forced herself to say.

She heard the ice cubes in his glass clink against each other. She swirled her own drink. That was much more interesting for the cherry than just tilting it, anyway.

"Work was so tough today. How I envy you, being able to stay at home. Not having to deal with those idiots at the office."

Envy.

"Yeah."

"It's so good knowing you're here, waiting for me to come home. It makes the hours bearable until I get to come through that door and sit in this chair."

"You don't seem to be so worried about work when you leave in the morning."

"No?" If he picked up the edge, the shards of frost in her voice, he didn't comment. "Well, I'm still half-asleep in the morning, darling. You know that. And I certainly don't look forward to work every day. But I do have to do it, and I suppose I think about it in the morning, before I go. It's better than thinking of how much I will be missing you."

"Is that what you think about? Work? When you're reading the paper in the morning?" She wanted to say *when you're hiding behind the paper*, but she didn't. She was already wandering into dangerous territory, questioning him at all. But if she was in that territory, she wanted to be slinking in, hiding, not rushing in blaring a trumpet and clanging cymbals.

"Oh, I suppose so. Work and the news. I think about them both, I guess. All that. Boring stuff to you, I'm sure. Nothing for you to worry about." There was a pause. Sharon assumed he was taking another drink, but she stayed fixated on her own. "It's sweet of you to think of me, though, Sharon, and think about what I'm thinking about."

"Yeah."

She tilted her head back and swallowed her drink in one gulp. Small though it was, it burned, and she spluttered. Tears sprang to her eyes.

"That's a little unnecessary, don't you think?"

"What?" Sharon coughed.

"Downing your drink like that."

Sharon finally looked at her husband again. He was looking at her, eyebrows raised. He didn't look angry or annoyed, she realized. He looked amused.

She'd have preferred him being angry.

She stared at him as she tilted her glass again, capturing the cherry in her mouth. It burst between her teeth, sweet and tart and tasting of the vermouth more than the whiskey, which struck Sharon as a little odd. She strode to the bar cart and set her glass down with a little more force than usual.

"Don't do that," he said, eyebrows still raised.

"Do what?"

"Clang your glass like that. It could break."

"The glass isn't going to break."

"It might. You don't know. Are you a glass manufacturer? A structural engineer?"

"No."

"No, you aren't. So just don't clang the glasses. Be careful, and they won't break. Nice glasses like that, they can last a lifetime. Just have to be careful is all."

"Right." Sharon folded her hands in front of her. Her fingernails dug into her skin, hard enough to turn her hands white, hard enough to imprint, but not hard enough to cut. She started to bite her lip, but stopped, and breathed deep instead. "Sorry. I'll try to be more careful."

"Good. That's all I ask." He drank again, but Sharon turned and was already down the hall when the glass reached his lips. "Where are you going?" he asked after a moment.

She was already in the kitchen.

Good lord, Sharon thought. *Humanly. Where does he think I'm going? Where could I possibly be going?*

"Just in the kitchen," she called over her shoulder. *Always in the kitchen.* "Your supper's almost ready."

CHAPTER 14

6:00 pm

Supper was on the table before the clock on the wall chimed six times.

There was a cuckoo clock in Sharon's parents' living room. A big, wooden piece that stood in the corner. When things got bad at home, when her father was too loud and too scary, she'd sit herself in front of that clock, cross-legged until her mother caught her and scolded her for not being ladylike. After that, she'd kneel, her legs a little to the side, or she'd move to a chair and cross her legs at her ankles. But until then, cross-legged, every time, her elbows on her knees, her chin in her hands, watching the clock's hands move around its face, listening to the ticks and tocks and waiting for the sing-song chime of the half hour. The highlight was every hour, though, when the tiny double wooden doors would open, and the little painted bird launched itself out of its home. When she was very small, Sharon clapped and giggled with each appearance of that bird. Six o'clock meant six chimes, six thrusts into the open for the bird, six squeals and six claps from the little girl sitting and watching.

Much later, when she was in high school and she first figured out what was the matter with her, when her monthly pains changed and she started throwing up in the mornings, she sat in front of the clock again. But this time there was no squealing, no clapping. She was too old for that. This time she just watched the clock and waited for the bird.

And, when the seconds and minutes ticked and tocked away enough, and the bird finally made its appearance, Sharon's stomach flipped and twisted around the morning sickness. She brushed at her eyes, and the back of her hand came away wet. Birds weren't supposed to be trapped in wooden clocks, after all, no matter how intricate the carvings, no matter how detailed the paintings. Birds weren't supposed to be glued to little wooden diving boards, weren't supposed to spring forward or bob on cue, weren't supposed to be yanked backward after only a brief moment in the air.

Something in her gut made her want to reach through those little doors and free the bird. She wanted to tear the bird from its perch, snap that board into two or three or twelve little pieces. She wanted to rip off the little doors, throw something into the grinning, mocking face, smash and crush the whole clock and grind it all underfoot. She wanted to release the bird to the air and the wind and the clouds and destroy its wooden cage, its prison.

She knew that was all foolish, pointless. She even knew that her sadness wasn't even about the clock or the bird.

Not really.

She never did any of that. She dried her eyes, straightened her shoulders, and picked herself up from the floor. She smoothed her skirts and her hair, and went on to face the day and the decisions she made.

She never sat in front of that clock again, but now, dolloping a spoonful of butter on the top of the mixed vegetables, Sharon thought of that clock, and that bird. *Today does seem to be a day for birds,* she thought, watching the steam rise from the potatoes and vegetables. She pulled the foil away from the meatloaf just as Albert came to the table. They sat down, bowed their heads, and Sharon didn't close her eyes. After Albert finished saying their nightly thanks for their nightly meal, he started loading his plate.

Sharon watched and remembered her own parents. Her mother always dished up plates from the stove for her father, herself, her siblings. Then her father would be served the hottest meal possible.

Her mother always ate last. She spent most meals up and down, refilling plates, the water pitcher, picking up a dropped fork, spooning food into the younger children's mouths. Only later, when there was no more steam rising from her plate, when gravies and sauces started to congeal and soups had a thin skin-like layer, was she able to pick up her own fork.

At least Albert didn't expect her to do that. He could dish up his own plate, at least, from the serving dishes in front of him. Dishes she'd dusted, filled with food she'd cooked and prepared.

A little head shake cleared her mind of these troublesome thoughts. *The whole day,* she scolded, *I've been thinking things I shouldn't be thinking. And why? Just because of some dream about some boy?*

But she knew there was more to her thinking and wondering and worrying than just some dream she'd woken with. More to her time at the hospital today, more to her conversations with Bonnie and Melinda, more to her rememberings about her family and her former classmates and James, and even more to her memories about… well, about that time, that time she was sick.

Her hand dropped to her stomach, rested there a moment.

Another head shake to clear her mind. *Troublesome thoughts, indeed.* She realized where her hand was and pulled it away, reaching instead for the gravy.

"You okay, darling?" Albert spooned potatoes onto his plate. Sharon held the gravy boat toward him.

"What?"

"You're shaking your head. You've done that a fair bit lately." Another spoonful of potatoes.

"Have I?" Sharon forced a smile, realized her lips were pressed together again, and tried to soften her face. Her arm was getting sore from the gravy. "Sorry, dear."

"So long as you're okay." A third spoonful, then at last he set aside the potatoes and turned his attention to the bowl Sharon held in front of him.

She felt a little lightheaded, as she had at the hospital that morning, and again staring at the tree while hanging laundry. Resisting the urge to shake her head again, though, she smiled wider at her husband. Her cheeks ached from the tension there. He put down the gravy bowl, picked up his fork, and dug into his pile of food. She picked up her fork too, but also her knife, and spent more than a minute cutting her meatloaf into tiny bite-size squares. Only then did she start to eat, little bites, chewing each one ten times, as her mother had taught her.

She only ate with such precision when Albert was around.

For a while there was no sound other than the scrape of forks and knives against the plates and the sound of Albert chewing.

"Gosh darned good, Sharon. Gosh darned good."

She swallowed before answering him. "Thank you, dear."

Her eyes followed his fork as he wiggled it against his meatloaf to hack off a piece, then stab the meat, run it through the pile of mashed potatoes, dip that mixture into his gravy, and shovel the whole hodgepodge into his mouth.

She wondered if he would recognize the hint if she stared at his knife, or perhaps at the napkin resting by his plate and definitely not across his lap.

At least he chews with his mouth closed, Sharon thought, dabbing her own mouth with the corner of her napkin.

When she looked at him again, her eyes widened and she flinched. He was watching her.

He swallowed. His Adam's apple slid up and down, prominent enough for Sharon to see from her seat at the table without looking too hard.

"You aren't eating?"

And at least he doesn't talk with his mouth full.

She gave him another quick smile. "I'm eating. Just not a lot. I don't have much of an appetite, I guess."

"You okay?"

"You already asked me that, dear." She sipped from her water glass. "I told you I was fine."

"I know you said that." He shifted his focus to his plate, scooped up another meatloaf - potato - gravy concoction, and spilled half of it in the space between the plate and his mouth.

Sharon averted her gaze, picked up her fork, and slid around the precise meatloaf pieces.

"You sure you're okay? Head shaking, not eating... I know you said you're fine, but I just want to make sure. If you aren't feeling well, we can make an appointment with the doctor."

"I've been to the doctor." The words were out before she realized it, parading their way across the table to her husband. Her cheeks flamed, and she bit her lip, cleared her throat.

This was it. This was the moment she'd promised herself would come. Even this morning, when she'd determined to tell him, this was how she imagined it, sitting in the kitchen, at the table. *Darling, I have to tell you something…*

Now all she had to do was say it. Open her mouth and let the words tumble out. Just tell him, quick, get it done with. He'll understand.

"Oh? When was that?"

This was a moment, one of those open invitations where they could talk. But even as the thought tiptoed across her mind, peeking around corners and in the shadows, she closed off that possibility. She knew they wouldn't talk, knew she couldn't tell him.

She wouldn't.

Telling him the truth now, after all, could somehow lead to telling him the truth about before. If she told him about those symptoms, that butterfly feeling, that running to empty her stomach every morning, she couldn't tell him that it was all familiar to her. If she did, there would be questions. How did she know? More to the point, why didn't she tell him about it?

And why did things turn out the way they had? That was another question, one for which she had no answer.

One for which she was afraid of the answer.

Was it because of before? The last time? The… the illness? The decision? The…? No. No, she wouldn't wonder. Wouldn't even think about it.

And she wouldn't talk to Albert about it, either.

"Yesterday." She tilted her head and sighed, choosing her course of action. "Come on, dear. Surely you remember. I told you about it in the morning. And the night before as well, I believe."

"You did?"

127

"Of course I did." She raised her eyebrows. "Not to mention when I first made the appointment."

"I don't remember that."

She pushed out another sigh.

"Well, I'm sorry," he continued. "I just don't remember."

She debated rolling her eyes, but worried that would maybe be a little too much. "Honestly, Albert. I wish you would pay attention when I tell you these things. I know how busy you are, but I don't think it's too much to ask for you to remember a few appointments when I tell you about them."

"I usually do remember. That's why I'm confused now."

She dipped her head. The trick now was to smile that small smile he loved, to widen her eyes, soften them somehow, look up at him with all the love of a good wife forgiving her silly, forgetful husband. "Yes, dear. You're right. Usually you do. You just didn't this time."

Albert didn't respond, and Sharon worried he had figured out her ruse, she had gone too far, stepped out of her place. Her gaze dropped, and she slid her food from one side of the plate to the other.

Her mouth dried behind the small smile she maintained. She cleared her throat. It didn't help. She reached for her water, gulped some down past the lump forming in the back of her throat.

She chanced a glance at Albert. He was still watching her.

Oh no.

She reached for her glass again. Another gulp down. Still, Albert said nothing.

The silence weighing on her, she had to throw it off, had to break it, had to say something. "Dear," she finally said, clearing her throat before continuing, "I'm sorry for criticizing you. That wasn't right. It isn't my place to do that. I guess maybe I must not be feeling so well after all."

He sniffed.

"In fact," she continued, rushing now to fill that empty, silent space between them, "I suppose I do feel a bit of a headache coming on. That must be it."

"Hmm."

Albert didn't say anything more than that one guttural sound, but he did shift his attention to his plate again, and pushed his fork through the mess of gravy and potatoes. Sharon sighed, a mixture of relief and nausea slipping through her veins, from the roots of her hair, through every inch of skin beneath her dress, that dress that could blend into the neighbor's home. The hair on her arms stood up, and, seeing this, she dropped her hands to her lap, folding them there.

"You should eat something, Sharon." His words were to her, his attention to the potatoes. "Might help your headache."

No "darling", no pet name. Just Sharon.

"Yes, dear."

And so she picked up her fork, ignoring her puckered and pimpled skin, and forced her hand to bring a half-forkful to her lips, her eyes downcast, wondering if she'd crossed a line somewhere between husband and wife, between proper and improper, between playing a game and losing.

CHAPTER 15

7:00 pm

The rest of the meal was quiet, a quiet free of conversation, but also of criticism. Sharon took twelve more bites. She counted each. Twelve more bites, ten mechanical chews for each. One hundred twenty journeys up and down for her jaw, her teeth.

That was what she focused on, not on the way Albert had looked at her, eyes open, blinking slowly, no expression behind them. One hundred and twenty. Not the silence stretching and coiling itself around the table, around the meatloaf, around them. One hundred and twenty.

At last he looked away from her, shoveling that meatloaf - potato - vegetable - gravy concoction into his mouth. He sure didn't chew each bite ten times.

She didn't mind though; if he was eating her food, everything was fine. And truly, perhaps everything was fine. Perhaps she was just being overly sensitive to the silence, the stare.

She broke that silence once, to ask if Albert was finished, if he wanted dessert.

"Yes, darling."

His eyes were on the sink, and Sharon was torn. Had she tidied it enough after preparing the meal? But still, her heart fluttered at that word, *darling*.

He must not be angry, not truly, not really.

She carried the dishes to the sink, the food, securing each in the little plastic containers with the little light green plastic lids.

Those lids could almost blend with her dress and the neighbor's house, too.

She wished she'd made something more substantial for dessert, but it was too late for that now. She spooned vanilla ice cream into bowls, added a cookie from the beehive-shaped cookie jar to his, and set it in front of him. She laid the spoon beside the bowl, and when she reclaimed her seat, her own, much smaller bowl of ice cream before her, Albert turned his attention from her to his dessert.

She tried a spoonful. It was cold, and tasted of childhood and adolescence, of summers sitting on her grandparents' front porch and afternoons giggling with Melinda. She and James used to share bowls of ice cream at Macney's. One bowl, two spoons. And they would talk and smile and just be there together, in the kind of love that wallops you over the head, the kind of love characteristic of teenagers and first loves.

With Albert, there had been no head-walloping.

She took another spoonful of ice cream

No, Albert was never the kind of love that hit that hard and spontaneous. It was slow, a nudge, a whisper.

She didn't know which was better, but she did know both were real.

"Dear, I'm sorry," she said, after swallowing another spoonful.

He looked at her. Blinked. "For what?"

It was her turn to blink now. Could she really have been worried about his reaction for no reason? Could she really have been reading too much into his silence, his stares? "I... I spoke to you harshly a few moments ago."

"Oh. Yes. Well, there is no need to apologize, darling." His spoon scraped the side of the bowl. "You said you weren't feeling well, that you had a headache."

"Yes."

"Besides, you're right. Sometimes I don't pay enough attention to what you say. So perhaps I should be apologizing to you."

It wasn't an apology, not a real one, anyway. Yet it was at least the suggestion of one, for his imagined offense, so even though it was given with that self-assured smile, that eyebrow lift, Sharon smiled and thanked him, assuring him that all was well.

She just prayed that he wouldn't return to the conversation, asking about the doctor's appointment. If she could have crossed her fingers without him noticing, she would have. Instead, she crossed her legs at her ankles, the way her mother and her home economics and etiquette teacher, Mrs. Smythe, had taught her.

Instead, he asked about the hospital visit.

Letting out her breath in a spluttering cough, she nodded, spooning a bit more of the ice cream into her mouth. It was starting to melt, and she spooned up another before it morphed entirely into soup.

"It was good," she said, when she'd swallowed, the cold both soothing and burning her throat. "I mean, it was fine. Things like that aren't exactly good, you know."

"Sure."

She looked down at her bowl. Almost soup. She had another spoonful anyway, the taste and texture bringing her thoughts back to a booth in Macney's, and she shot her eye back up to Albert as she swallowed.

"There was this little boy. Is, I guess. I mean, he's still there I'm sure. I'm pretty sure." She knew she was babbling, wished she wasn't, then forged ahead anyway. "He's adorable, you know. His hair is like feathers. Anyway, he always is the one who gets to pick out the book for me to read."

"Why?"

She blinked. "Why what?"

"Hardly seems fair to the other kids, always letting the same kid pick out a book each time. Why not give everyone a turn?"

"Oh." She looked down again. "I hadn't really thought of that. He picks books for others sometimes." An image of a book with a ballerina on the cover flittered behind her eyelids, but she swept it away. "And they don't seem to mind him choosing."

"Hmm."

Not a word, just that syllable, emanating from somewhere between his chest and his throat, and it was enough to pause Sharon. Without thinking, her mind and body made minute recalibrations. Her posture straightened, her chin lifted, her shoulders squared. Her voice quieted, rounded. Her forehead smoothed, her eyebrows softened, her eyes dimmed.

"Yes." Her speech was slower, more considered. "I will think about that more carefully in the future."

"Good. Now. What about this kid?"

"Oh." She shifted a little, moving her weight from hip to hip in her seat. She uncrossed, then re-crossed her ankles. She had been on the verge of telling him something. She could picture the words pouring from her as though she were a watering can and the words were water. She thought again of the tulips she'd contemplated.

Words, like water. Sometimes they nourished, quenched.

Other times they drowned.

"I just thought you may find it interesting to hear about one of the children in the ward."

"Of course, darling. Is he a handsome boy?"

"Yes."

"And well-behaved? At least that you can see?"

"Yes. He's always a perfect little gentleman." Here the corners of her lips twitched, and before she became aware of it, she was continuing. "He always offers his arm to walk me to the bookshelf, or around the room. I have to stoop so much to take it, of course. And he's always very polite. He has excellent manners." Her brain caught up with her mouth, and she stopped talking.

"Good. They must have teachers or something who come in to teach those kids how to behave."

"Yes. They must."

He nodded, seeming to approve of where his tax dollars went, or so Sharon assumed. She dropped her hands to her lap.

Albert's spoon clinked and clattered as he dropped it into the empty bowl, having finished the last of his ice cream soup.

"Are you finished, dear?"

"Yes, Sharon." When he smiled at her, really smiled, his whole face joined in. At first he always seemed surprised. His eyebrows rose, his eyes widened, and they always were directed at exactly what they found so amusing. His lips parted, just enough to reveal his teeth in perfect rows. Then it was like his face folded in on itself. His eyes crinkled, eyebrows and cheeks and dimples becoming a network of lines and creases that she knew would result in wrinkles sooner or later. Sooner, the way he was at it. His teeth, much more visible then, were framed by lips that seemed to spread across his whole face, from ear to ear.

He smiled at her in such a way then. "Thanks for dinner, darling. When I'm gone all day, you know, I just want to come home to you. I think about it a lot you know, coming in the door and sitting at this table, and you being here, and it's such a good thing, such a comfort to me."

What could she say? She blinked, and smiled her own response to him. "Thank you, Albert. I'm always happier when you're home, too."

That much was true.

She looked down and cleared her throat. She could say something else, now. Tell him something, throw him some rope and she could hold the other end and they could pull one another to themselves and then tie a big knot around them, together. Some knowledge, some word could be that rope.

"Albert, I…" She started, faltered, and looked up. He was watching her, almost staring, his head tilted a little, leaning forward, as though he knew something important was about to be said.

"I…" She tried again, then looked down, thinking that staring at her bowl, at the little pool of white melted there - *the colour of snow and innocence and the pearls she wore at her wedding* - was easier than staring into his dark eyes.

The answers, the words, weren't there either, so she cleared her throat, looked back at him. "I was wondering… if you're done, that is… I'll do the dishes."

He leaned back, and his smile shrank. He nodded, and her insides all slumped in on themselves. Except, of course, for the voice whispering the word *coward*.

If the voice reminding her to take care of the flower bed had been her mother's, this one sounded suspiciously like Melinda's.

She picked up their dishes, carried them to the sink and ran the water, added the soap. The white suds reminded her of her earlier thoughts, her rememberings of her classmate, Margot. And the remembering of that remembering sent another word whispering through her mind.

James.

She dipped the bowls into the hot water. She didn't put on gloves, relishing the shock and pain from the hot water.

Albert was still in his chair. Her back was to him, but she knew he hadn't moved, knew it from the lack of any other sound, more than any connection or supernatural ability on her part. There had been no scrape of his chair, no cough or shift as he stood, no muttering or humming or shuffling as he moved to the living room or his study.

Odd that he's still here. Perhaps it's a sign - is that something those hippies believed in? Signs? Is that part of that word? That Buddhism? No matter. Perhaps it is a sign that he wants to talk. To listen.

"Listen, Albert. There's something I want to talk about. Something we should talk about."

Yes, this is easier. She plunged her hands into the sink, grabbed a spoon, ran the sponge over the handle.

"Is there? And what's that?"

"With, with the hospital."

"Have you been working too hard? Do you want to stop your volunteer work?"

"No, dear." She found the other spoon, washed that one, too. "Just the opposite. I enjoy my time there. No, enjoy isn't the right word." She paused, her hands back in the water, still clutching the spoon. "It isn't that I enjoy it. It's that... It's important. I do good there."

"Of course you do, darling."

"And I... " - *How to make him understand?* "I want to do more of it."

"More volunteer hours? That shouldn't be a problem..."

"No," she interrupted. "That's not what I mean. I want to... I want to finish my nursing. I want to be there all the time. I want to work in a hospital."

There. It was out now, and she couldn't take it back. The words were hovering in the air, little clouds floating around, beneath the ceiling tiles and the chandelier.

There was no response, save the ticking of the clock from the living room.

Seconds stretched by. Sharon was afraid to disturb the silence as the silence stretched to one minute, then two. She didn't so much as shift her hands, afraid of the sloshing the water would make.

The clouds her words made were heavy. Would there be a shower in them or a torrential flood? Words were like water, she reminded herself. The question now was whether hers would quench or drown.

The silence became even heavier. The weight, the clouds, were crushing. At last, she could stand it no further.

"You see, I had a doll when I was a little girl." She rushed ahead. "She was always sick. I always pretended she was sick. And it would be my job to fix her. And I could, you know, that was the trick. I wanted to help her, and I want to help others, real kids, and adults too, of course. Not just kids." She took a breath, tried to calm her heart, tried to quiet the blood rushing in her ears. "What I mean is, I've always wanted to help sick people. I can do that as a nurse."

"You don't think you do that now?" Albert's words were slow, measured with time and thought, but there was no anger lurking on the edges of his syllables.

"I do. I do, I know I do." A breath in, a breath out. "I mean… Well, I can do more. I want to do more."

"Did you ever think…" He paused, and her back stiffened. But he continued, in his same careful, quiet tone. "I am so proud of you. And you're right; you do so much for the people you visit in the hospital. You don't have to do that, any of that, but you do. And I think you're good at it. I'm sure you are. You want to make a difference, to be important."

"Yes. That's right." She was afraid to turn around, afraid to find out the destination this path this conversation was heading down.

"You already do that. You make a difference to the people you see there. You're important to them. And I think you are so wonderful for that. Like I said, I'm so proud of you. I mean it. You're so good and selfless. And so smart. You're right about that too. If you went to finish your nursing… You're smart enough to do that. A lot of girls pretend to be dumber than they really are. One of the things I love about you is that you never do that."

This time she was quiet.

"I think, though, if you went to work, really went to work… well, do you really want to do that?"

"What do you mean?"

"Do you want to have those hours, that stress? Do you want to give up your days? Even for the hospital; you couldn't go visit whoever you want so much, couldn't read to the kids the way you do. That little boy, you wouldn't see him so much.

Especially when we have our own kids. Do you want to start working just to quit your job when we start a family?"

Still, she was quiet.

Even her mind was quiet. Albert was not saying anything she hadn't thought of before, not saying anything she hadn't expected him to say the countless times she imagined this conversation.

But his tone was unexpected. Quieter, softer, more thoughtful.

"I know you want a home, a family. To be here with me. You do want that, don't you?"

"Yes." Her response was whispered, immediate. Automatic.

"So do you really want to work, too? Be a nurse? Leave the house every day to clock in at a job?"

Sharon flinched at the way he said that word, job, like the three little letters tasted badly. He spat them out, as though he was disgusted, as though the word was sour milk.

"Is that what you want?"

"Yes." Again, her response was whispered. But this time, something else whispered too, something in her veins, in the recesses of the blood pumping through her - *as outlined on pages 22 and 23* of the text, she thought to herself - and she was compelled to continue. "At least, I think so."

"I see."

This time she did hear his chair creak, the unmistakable sound of her husband shifting his weight in his seat. She moved too, sliding a plate into the suds and swirling the sponge along it, clearing off those little blue flowers along the edge.

She didn't know what more to say. She had been honest. Honest about this, anyway. About the rest, the other part, she hadn't said. She wouldn't say. Couldn't. Anytime the conversation shifted to family, to children, she faltered.

Would she have to choose? In all of her imaginings, she hadn't thought Albert would entertain, even discuss, the possibility of her actually becoming a nurse, actually working. And now, was he asking her what she really wanted?

But it wasn't so simple as picking which way to turn down a path at a crossroads. There wasn't a sign pointing the right direction.

"Have you considered…" There was a cough, and Sharon twisted the sponge again around the plate, now clean, still in her soapy hand. She waited for Albert to continue.

"Have you thought, I mean, that maybe you could finish your nursing studies and then not be a nurse? You're so smart. You could finish it all, and then continue choosing your own hours, your own dates for work, for volunteer work, at the hospital. What do you think of that?"

She remembered the conversation that had already drifted through her recollections once this same day, of a low conversation in bed one night, words meant to her husband but spoken to the wall and the ceiling and the dark.

"I don't know. Maybe…"

"I think it would be great for you to be a nurse, if that's what you really want. But maybe it's not. Only what you think you want."

Sharon felt hot and cold and wondered how she could be both at the same time.

The clouds that had been gathering in the room opened up, and she felt the rain cloud her vision. If she was at a crossroads, the rain was heavy enough she couldn't see down either path.

"Why don't you finish your school stuff? Keep volunteering. Use your knowledge for our kids one day. It would be helpful, be good for them. And then, when they are older, all grown up, if you still really want to go to work and be a nurse, you can do that then."

The plate went back into the water. She flattened her palms against the inside of the sink, the water up to the freckle on her forearm. Again, she followed the breathing formula from her childhood. *In. Out. In. Out.*

"I really think it is the best of both worlds. All worlds." Another creak, another chair shift. "What do you think, darling?"

"Um…" *In. Out. In. Out. Blink away the rain,* she told herself. *Pick the path. He's probably right. Maybe this way you can do both.* She imagined herself walking down the path leading to a swingset in the corner of the yard. Albert believed she could retrace her steps, pick her way back years later, and move down the other one, leading to a hospital and that white nurse's uniform.

White. *Snow and innocence and the pearls she wore to her wedding.*

"I think… I'll think about it. You may be right."

"I think I am." A louder creak, a scrape; she knew he was getting up. "Think about it, though. Consider it. We can talk about it later."

"Yes, dear."

"I'm going into the living room. I was thinking we could do something together tonight. How about that puzzle my mother got you for Christmas?"

"Sounds lovely, dear."

His steps, heavy, grew louder. Then he was behind her, his hands on her shoulder, easing her back against him

She yielded, leaning back that traction, closing the space between him. His being, his presence, his chest was broad and strong, as encompassing and solid and steady as his hands on her shoulders.

She felt his breath on the top of her head, felt him drop a kiss in her hair, and she closed her eyes.

And then he moved away, and her shoulders, her body was lighter, but also emptier.

"Finish the dishes, darling, and come soon. I'll even make us our drinks."

His footsteps softened, receded.

"Yes, dear," she answered to the empty room.

CHAPTER 16

8:00 pm

The puzzle was one of those complicated ones with a hundred shades of blue and yellow and white. Water and sky, a boardwalk, sailboats lined up at a pier.

Albert had the box sitting on the coffee table when she came in the room. As promised, two drinks waited, one a dark amber in front of him, and another, much paler, opposite him.

She opened the box, shook out the pieces, spread them across the table, and flipped them up so the image was evident.

No, not the image. The colours. The image was far from discernible; only the colours were there, those snippets of snippets, pieces of pieces.

The border first. Figure out the outline of what she wanted, what they wanted, then fill in the rest.

A puzzle again. Was it really only this morning that she'd been considering her life, her... illness... and her recovery from it, as a puzzle?

Find the pieces, force them together. Cut them, file them off if you have to. Just fit it together. So long as the picture more or less makes sense, at least from a distance.

The house was a puzzle piece. Albert. The washing machine. The new items ordered from the salesman. The green dress that matched the neighbor's house. It all fit together, it all made a picture that looked pretty good, so long as you didn't look too close, as long as you didn't see the uneven edges, the raised corners.

The tension in her shoulders relaxed as they fit pieces together. Conversation was light, sporadic, superficial, and comfortable. Easy, even.

They shared this task, passing one another the colours, working together in hope the image would reveal itself.

No, that wasn't quite right. She glanced at Albert, at his head, bent, tilted, studying the image on the box. They weren't sitting back, hoping an image would magically reveal itself and make sense. They were making the picture fit together, making it make sense.

He did that. Even when she didn't want the piece, didn't need it, he passed it to her, helped her to fit together the outline, the foundation, the waves and the little row of houses and their lives.

Their life. Singular. One life.

He helped her find where the pieces went. He helped her make them fit.

It wasn't unhappy. She wasn't even angry, except at herself. She wanted to tell him, wanted to talk to him, to air her secrets out like she aired the laundry every day. She wanted to work, and she told him that. But yesterday's appointment; she'd wanted to tell him that. She wanted him to know the fear and worry and apprehension and confusion sitting in that waiting room, then lying back on that examination table. She wanted him to hate the shaking doctor's head, that pity look in his eyes, just as she did. She wanted him to understand. But how could he? She didn't. She didn't understand anything except the frustration and the confusion and the terrible, pulling, aching inside her that weighed in her very marrow and whispered to her that it was all her fault, that shaking head, those pitying eyes.

The other secret, the big one, that she could never tell him.

And instead, she let the guilt sit deep in her, eating away at her, condemning herself to more unwelcome visitors in unwelcome dreams, while she sat here completing a puzzle.

She worked on the blue corner, and Albert passed her pieces when they didn't fit the sky he was working on.

Her fingers hovered over one such piece. She turned it around, studied it, furrowed her brows at it, wondered at the black speck there.

"Oh." She handed it to her husband. "This one belongs to you. It's a part of the sky."

"It is? Are you sure?"

"Quite sure." She fit another piece, a small wave, in place. She focused her attention on her little corner of their puzzle world, but cast a casual glance at him and smiled, swallowing at air and something else she didn't recognize or understand. "It's part of a bird."

"Huh." He plucked it from her hand, turned it one way, then the other, upside-down, sideways, right-side-up.

"Guess I didn't recognize it."

CHAPTER 17

9:00 pm

They had another drink together. This one Sharon poured. Hers was a darker amber than the one Albert made her, but it wasn't so dark as the last one she'd made herself that afternoon.

After almost an hour, Albert became restless. She could tell in the way he shifted, the way he sat back, the way he swirled his glass, the ice cubes clinking against one another and the sides of the glass.

That's when she'd pressed her hands to her knees, rose, and gathered their glasses, refreshing their drinks without asking.

Moments after taking the first sips from this new drink, he cleared his throat and rose himself.

"Darling, would you mind terribly if I excused myself for a bit? There's some work I ought to do tonight. I'd much rather be out here with you than in my study, of course. And I did tell you we would spend time together tonight, so if you'd really rather I stay, then I will. My papers can wait until tomorrow evening. If that's what you wish, of course. It's up to you."

Her eyes met his. What work was it that he just had to do in his study? What papers? She knew of no work that he brought home, no work that he had to complete behind that closed door at night.

Well, everyone is entitled to his - or her - own secrets.

"Of course, dear," she said, dropping her eyes again to the coloured cardboard in her hand. "Work away. I think I'll continue with this for a bit more."

"Sounds nice. Why don't you leave it out and maybe we can finish it tomorrow?"

"Yes, dear. Sure."

He waited, hovering over her and the coffee table with the half-finished row of houses and gathering of sailboats. Other pieces, the misfits searching for their places, were strewn about the vacant spaces.

There was something more. The air was heavy with it, that unknown anticipation of what he might say. He opened his mouth, sighed, and his tongue slipped over his lips. She wondered what he was going to add to their conversation, their night, her day.

But he seemed to reconsider. He closed his mouth and just nodded, one simple bob of his head, then left, taking his drink with him.

When he left the air seemed lighter. The clouds from the kitchen, the rain, had cleared with their first drink and the time spent on the puzzle. But it still hung in the air, weighted on her skin and the top of her hair where he'd kissed her. Her skin was damp and heavy with it.

She leaned forward, wrapping one arm around her stomach while the other rested on her knee, her drink balancing between those fingertips, shifting back and forth. Her eyes slid over the puzzle. She picked up a piece, tried it in a space.

No luck.

She moved it over to another space, and tried again.

No.

She could have told him about the doctor's appointment while she was being honest, she knew. She would never tell him about the past, about that procedure, that illness, her time with Melinda.

About James.

But she could have told him about the appointment. She could have found a way to avoid the symptoms, or rather, her recognition of the symptoms. She could have said Bonnie suggested it, maybe. The nausea in the morning, the loss of appetite, the exhaustion. If she'd told all of that to Bonnie, if she'd feigned innocence and naivete, then Bonnie would certainly have suggested it anyway. That was believable enough.

But was there a point, now?

She'd made the appointment, but the cramps, the blood, cleaned and hidden from Albert, had erased the possibility, and when she had kept the appointment, days later, the doctor had confirmed what she already knew.

She had been pregnant. Again.

And now she wasn't.

Again.

But the loss was different this time.

Different, but no less secret.

She couldn't tell Albert. What if he thought she'd done something that led to the loss? What if she'd driven over a bump, or eaten something she shouldn't have, or stumbled, or lifted something heavy? What if her time volunteering at the hospital had affected things? And what if he told her she couldn't do that anymore?

What if she hadn't done any of those things, hadn't done anything wrong at all, and what if he still blamed her? What if he criticized, if he yelled? Or, even worse, but so much more characteristic, what if he didn't? What if he held onto an unvoiced blame, wrapping it and burying it within himself to unearth and unwrap and shove under her nose in every heated argument throughout the rest of their lives?

Albert wasn't a bad man; she never believed he was. But he wouldn't understand. His eyes would see rattles and cribs and that would be their lives from now on. No, not their lives. Her life. He was happy in his world and his reality and maybe would see this as just a setback, a minor bump on their way - no, her way - to a big bump and parenthood. No, he wasn't unfeeling or unsupportive. Just the opposite.

He wouldn't yell.

He would be sympathetic. But maybe not just sympathetic; what if he pitied her? That was worse than the criticism. So much worse. What if he took her in his arms and ran his hand up and down her back and petted her hair and murmured soothing words?

What if he thought the desire she voiced tonight, to be a nurse, was to find some purpose, lost with the doctor's shaking head and clots and blood? What if he was right about that? What if there was something missing in her identity, her self, an emptiness that needed to be filled, or enriched? Was wanting to be a nurse her attempt to fill that emptiness? Was little Henry, reaching his hand out with his choice of picture book, another attempt?

And what if he was right about more? What if it *had* been something she did? Except not something she did now; what if it

149

was something she did before? Not that Albert would know that, of course. But what if her decision, from when James cheated and then left and she visited Melinda and thought she was going to die... what if that affected this pregnancy, now?

It could have been that, she knew.

The knowledge sat in her, heavy, hard, cold, an ice chunk, with cutting, slicing edges.

No, this was too tied up within her to belong to him. It was another of her secrets, another frozen burden.

What if the ice never melted? What if it froze her forever? Or what if it did melt, if it washed her all out and left her shivering and empty?

She fit in another puzzle piece. This one clicked into place, neat, clean, like the corners of the sheets of a hospital bed.

Time would tell. It was the only thing that would tell.

Even if the ice never melted. Or if it did. Even if she could never have children, if that illness and vertigo never resulted in anything else, she knew that the money she'd paid to that doctor, the feverish days, even the fear of dying, was her reality. It was the decision she made, and so the ice was worth it.

She didn't know if it was the right choice. But neither did she know of any other option available.

A life with ice, with this secret, this knowledge, was better than what it would have been on her own, with no money, no family, shunned, abandoned, with someone else she couldn't care for.

The choice was made. She hadn't wanted to have to... Even now, she couldn't say the words. Couldn't even think them. But she hadn't wanted to make that choice. Hadn't wanted to *have* to make that choice. But neither did she regret it.

Even if it froze her.

She raised her glass to her lips. Took another drink.

I sure seem to be drinking a lot today.

What life would it have been for her, let alone someone else? No tie to her past, fumbling and struggling through the present, and no future.

And that was if her father didn't get so angry that he hurt her. Even if she had been allowed to stay at home, how could she bring someone else into that house? Especially someone else so vulnerable? If the price for that was having to live with this ice in her, hard, cutting, freezing, then so be it.

That was her consequence.

So how could I tell Albert now, about this loss?

The puzzle was incomplete. Enough had been put together to see the picture, but there were gaps, vacancies. It was incomplete, unfinished.

She didn't try to force any of these pieces. Let that happen in her real life; this picture will keep.

It will wait.

She leaned back, collapsing against the back of the couch cushions, and tipping back her glass again. The drink was warm and sweet.

Moving her arm away from her stomach and resting it on the seat beside her, she cast her attention across the coffee table.

She didn't have to complete it all tonight. She could figure it out later. Tomorrow, or the next day.

Or the next.

There was time.

Nothing but time.

CHAPTER 18

10:00 pm

Sharon decided not to wash their drink glasses that night. Hers waited by the sink, Albert's in his study. Of course he wasn't going to bring it out with him when he reappeared. She looked forward to the excuse to go get it, to trespass in his domain. Perhaps she would leave it for a while, allow it to collect a thin layer of dust so when she did at last retrieve it, there would be a small ring, a small remnant of itself left behind. And perhaps she would leave that for a while, too.

Disappointment gnawed at her. She was disappointed in herself, in her reaction, that she looked forward to something as small as retrieving a glass, that she felt so much a stranger in his study that venturing into it was trespassing.

And she was disappointed that she wouldn't actually let dust collect there. She wouldn't leave a glass ring. Of course she wouldn't. She wouldn't stay away from his domain, from him. And that voice in her head, the same one that whispered at her to look after the front flower borders, the one that sounded suspiciously like her mother's, she wouldn't - couldn't - ignore that, either.

Each glass was left in each one's most significant place, his and her true home within the home, she realized. Their hooks on the wall, their glasses, their smears and lip marks, their melted ice cubes, all traces of each of them claiming their territories, their "thereness".

When she set the glass down she was struck with the overwhelming possibility of sliding it across the counter. If she spun it, if she slid it, if she picked it up and hurled it to the floor, the counter, against the cupboard, so it smashed, what would happen?

During their before-supper drinks he'd reminded her to be careful setting down the glasses. What would he say if she broke one?

She imagined it shattering into smithereens, shards scattering across the floor. The sound would be a crashing explosion, and tiny fractals of glass would reflect the light from the ceiling, creating a kaleidoscope across the vinyl floor.

She could smash those pieces even further. If she was daydreaming, she may as well take it even further. She could crush the shards underfoot into fine powder. Of course, she'd need to go get shoes for that.

Or not.

On those best and worst days at the hospital, sometimes she thought similar thoughts driving home. There was a bit of a hill around one corner, right before the road crossed the railroad tracks. More than once she'd wondered what it would feel like to steer right off the road down that hill.

Would it feel like flying?

And a couple months ago, when she was stopped at the crossing, waiting for a train to pass, she'd imagined herself driving into its side. All it would take is shifting her foot to the gas. The slightest movement, the slightest pressure.

Her heart hammered just thinking about it.

Of course those were only thoughts. She didn't drive into the train, and she didn't fly off the road and down the hill.

And she wouldn't smash the glass to the floor.

She'd just have to clean it up anyway.

*   *   *

Sharon stared at her reflection in the mirror above the sink. Her hands slid the brush down her hair, and she blinked away her mother's voice and her mother's hands from her memory. Instead, she focused on her eyes. Before long there would be lines there, in the corners. She shifted her head to the left, then the right. Little lines formed over years of laughing and crying and squinting and frowning and smiling.

She used to try to brush her hair one hundred times a night. Her mother said that was good for her hair, but even when she brushed it for her, neither sat still long enough to make it to one hundred. Eighty-three strokes was the furthest she'd ever counted before she got bored and let her mind wander and then get all mixed up and lose track of where she was in her counting.

Albert had already completed his nightly bathroom routine.

The lights were out in the hallway, and she heard him rummaging around in the bedroom. A dresser drawer opened and closed, footsteps rose and fell, bedsprings creaked and groaned.

She smoothed her nightgown over her hips and pulled her robe closed, tightening and tying the belt around her waist.

The hall lights were off already. Albert was always complaining about wasting electricity. So Sharon moved toward the bedroom in the dark.

He was reading when she got there. Not a newspaper; this was a western novel with a picture of rugged cowboy in hat and vest, a gun slung low on his hips, his arms held out at an angle as though he was about to draw his gun on whatever threat he saw off in the desert horizon.

She pulled back the covers and slipped into bed, feet stretching below the top sheet. She arranged her nightgown and then the covers on top, straightening them as she lay back.

The sheets felt cool to her feet, her arms. The pillow felt cool to her cheek.

She closed her eyes and sighed, letting the sheets and the quilt and the bed take away the hurt and heat from her day.

Another sound, and the bed dipped and creaked. There was a rustle of pages, then the quiet thump of a book being dropped onto a nightstand. Then a click, and the room filled with darkness. From behind her closed eyelids, Sharon welcomed it, let it seep into her.

Let this day be done, she implored the dark. *Let me sleep. Let me leave today behind.*

He was kissing her.

Her neck, her shoulder, her cheek. He was kissing her, and then there was another creak as he moved, and then he was over her.

She kept her eyes closed and said nothing, but her arms snaked around his neck, and she returned his kisses, and pulled him near, and for a while, she wasn't alone.

Afterward, she lay in his arms, her head in the hollow of his chest, the crook of his arm cradling her. Only then did she open her eyes.

She watched the rise and fall of his chest and rested her palm on the fine, soft hair curling there.

His fingers ran through her hair, separating strands, petting and combing. He stared at the ceiling, and she nestled closer.

"Darling," he said, "I was thinking about what you said after supper tonight. Do you think maybe we should start talking about children?"

Sharon froze. Cold slipped through her veins. "That wasn't exactly what I meant."

"Oh, I know that, darling. I was just thinking that maybe the time was coming for us to talk about it. We have been married a year now, after all."

"Eleven months."

"Right. Eleven months. Close enough. Almost a year."

"Almost." Her voice was quiet, breathy. She didn't trust it.

She flattened her palm on her chest.

"A year seems like a perfectly reasonable amount of time to at least be talking about it."

She said nothing. *In. Out. In. Out.* She counted eleven breaths, one for each month of their marriage.

"You're not wrong," she said at last. "I mean, I suppose you're right. It's a reasonable amount of time to talk about it."

"Yeah? And what do you think?"

Her heart tore at his tone. It was wistful and earnest and something about that questioning, that pleading, reminded her of little Henry, eyes wide, staring up at her.

Begging permission. Approval.

"I think... I mean, I don't know." She screwed her eyes shut and tried to continue. "What if we can't? You hear about that. Maybe the reason we aren't already... is because we can't. I can't. You never know." She opened her eyes again to the dark. "It could happen that way."

"Oh darling. No need to worry." The arm around her pulled her close, and he deposited a kiss on the top of her head. "That won't happen to us."

"How do you know?"

He shrugged, and the movement shifted her forward, then back. She settled in again and blinked away her dampening eyes. *Not now. Not now. Not now.*

No tears now. Only ice, please. Ice I can handle. Tears I can't.

"I just know," he murmured into her hair, and there was a finality to his voice that suggested the matter was closed, at least for now. Mother Nature or God or whoever sent the stork down to planet Earth with its precious cargo had better not thwart his plans. He sounded as a man who was used to getting his way, and Sharon both loved and hated that assuredness in him.

She wiggled back into her spot as he shifted again, and she swallowed her conflicting emotions, settling them in the pit of her stomach as her head settled on his chest.

"Besides," he continued, once more addressing the ceiling, "I would be okay with that."

Wait. What? He'd be okay with what?

"If you didn't have kids. If we didn't." His answer was quick enough that Sharon thought she may have spoken out loud.

"If we couldn't, I mean. Obviously we want kids."

"Obviously." This time her response was audible

"But if we couldn't have them. If that just never happened for us. I'd be okay with that." His arm squeezed her close, and she turned into it, burying herself in him. "I'd be okay with it just being us. Just you and me. That's all I need."

She didn't say anything. What could she say? Her heart ached and stretched and the pulse in her temples pounded.

157

She swallowed again. No word was sufficient. No word was big enough or small enough or true enough. She didn't know what to say, so she said nothing.

After a time, she heard the deep, slow breathing that signalled Albert's sleep. Just below a snore, open-mouthed.

In. Out. In. Out.

*   *   *

There was a romance novel on the nightstand by her side of the bed. She could open her eyes, disengage herself from Albert's arms, switch on her lamp, and read.

It was one of those "smut books" from her one shelf in Albert's study. The books all waited, tall, sentinels over all the goings-on of the room. She seldom visited the room and even more seldom took her books from that shelf, but this one she'd retrieved a couple weeks ago. One the cover there was a couple embracing in some sort of park, and judging from the disarray of their clothes and her hair, stylish though both were, it was rather windy. Her arms were around him, and she was smiling.

The woman in the book, Clarisse, had a love affair when she was younger. Maybe that's what drew Sharon to the book. Maybe she saw something of herself in that smiling woman.

Maybe she wanted to.

Maybe that's even why she had dreamt of James the previous night. Maybe it was more than the appointment the day before; maybe the words on the page reached back through her past and beckoned to the young man sitting there, waiting for her. "Go get him," the words had said to her subconscious, and her subconscious had found him and whispered, "Come with me."

That dream had set everything else off today. All day she'd been lost in her memories, struggling with her present realities.

And why? Because of some dream of some not-quite forgotten love? And why was there that dream? Because of some book? Because of a doctor shaking his head and that clutching in her chest whispering to tell Albert? To be honest?

The woman in the book had married someone else. Of course, she hadn't done what Sharon had. She hadn't made that decision. She hadn't had to. But she had moved on. And she found love. She found someone who fit her pieces back together, and she was busy, last Sharon left her, living a contented life with her dear, sweet husband.

It's not that simple. I can't ignore my past. I made the choices I made. And the choices I made, made me. They brought me here, with this man, in this home, in this life.

Right or wrong, that was it. This is it. This is me.

Those words tiptoed across her thoughts and slid down her veins and the skin of her arms and her belly and her legs. The bubbled up in her cells and in the darkness of the room and on all the hairs on her head.

She mouthed them. "Right or wrong."

The acceptance of it washed over her and through her. Still the words skipped inside. Perhaps the next day would bring the exact same routine, the same count of sips of coffee, the same order of making his breakfast and his footfalls in the hallway and the hours of watching the clock. Maybe it would bring visits with the neighbor, or a salesman, or someone at the hospital.

Maybe she would look at her nursing books.

Maybe she would read some of the recipes.

Maybe the hours would stretch in front of her and she would wash dishes and dust and sweep and put out the laundry again and again. Maybe she would fill the next day, and the one after that, and the one after that, with a million little tasks, little chores. Maybe the chunk of ice inside her would grow and grow and grow and freeze the blood in her veins and the beat of her heart.

But maybe not.

Maybe tomorrow, or one day, some day a month or a year or ten years from now, maybe things would be different.

Sharon flattened her palm again against Albert's chest. She would not turn to that book. Not tonight. Let that woman do what she would with her past love and her present husband.

She wasn't her.

Her past was real, as real as the money she paid that doctor, as real as the ache she felt in her bones at this new loss, as real as the way she warmed when Albert looked at her when he came home every day.

The whole day, the past had been following her, tapping her on the shoulder, shrinking into the shadows when she turned, then springing out at her around every corner of her day.

But my past is mine. Not James'. Not my mother's or my father's or Melinda's. Not even Albert's.

It is what it is. It was what it was.

She smiled, and though it wasn't quite a happy smile, neither was it a sad smile. It was sincere.

It all would be new again in the morning.

So let the smiling, embracing woman wait in her book a little longer. Sharon chose to have a good night's rest that night, unfettered by pesky dreams.

Beside her, beneath her, Albert slept.

She closed her eyes and breathed him in, matching her breathing to his inhalations and exhalations. The dark was a heavy blanket enveloped around her. She eased into it.

His chest rose and fell, and her head with it. She was wrapped up in this man, in his strength and his warmth and his frustration and his future, just as she was wrapped in his arms.

She didn't know whether he was sheltering her or suppressing her, but she chose to stay in his arms that night. *I'm both. Both constrained and protected.*

Held.

KRYSTA MACDONALD

A NOTE FROM THE AUTHOR

Mothers are interesting creatures. All parents are, of course, but there is something special about moms. This book tells the story of a mother, before she is a mother. In The Girl with Empty Suitcase, we followed Danielle, a window through whom the reader explored the way identity and relationships intertwine. One such relationship is rather complicated; the one with her mother.

But, like all people, there is another story behind the one we know. There is more to all people than that which we experience, and I wanted to know more about Danielle's mother before she was a mother. Who was she, this woman named Sharon? What was her reality?

What were her secrets?

I've always been interested in women's stories, especially the quiet stories. Especially the secret stories. It wasn't so long ago that women faced the same decisions and ramifications that Sharon did in her past; realities about reproduction and the complicated related decisions are still at the forefront of women's issues today. Yet, it is rarely discussed. Whether the loss of a pregnancy is a conscious choice or not, there are emotions connected that are difficult to talk about. In the past, we weren't really able to talk about it. Now, though, we can.

The women who struggle with these things, whether today or in the past, have stories, and this could be one.

ACKNOWLEDGEMENTS

When I was little, I wanted to be a writer. My thanks to my parents, siblings, grandparents, teachers, all who starred in these first attempts, supplied those crayons, dealt with my bookworm tendencies, and shaped me into who I am.

Thanks to Sharon Umbaug from The Writer's Reader, to my local novel writing group (Monica, Merilyn, and Joylene), to my beta readers (Corry, Diane, Lisa, Brandon), all of whom improved this manuscript and my writing.

A huge thank you goes to the talented cover artist, my mother-in-law, Karen MacDonald, who not only created the artwork but also fixed the disasters that came with transport and storage. Both my in-laws are so supportive of this and every endeavour.

Thank you to my friends and coworkers, who listen to updates and details and support my writing in so many ways. Thank you to my students, past and present, who remind me why I love the crazy effect of words on a page.

Finally, and most importantly, more thanks than I can ever express to my best friend and favourite human, who I get to share every day with. The second I thought I might want to write, my husband didn't question anything, just said, "Yes. You should." So I did. Every day since, he's been the same support, comfort and help. Thank you for being there for this adventure and every adventure. The words do not exist begin to express my thanks.

To all those who've read this and/or The Girl with the Empty Suitcase, thank you. Thank you for your comments and your time. And for those I've neglected to mention by name, my apologies and appreciation. So many of you have inspired and supported and just been plain awesome. Thank you.

ABOUT THE AUTHOR

Krysta MacDonald writes about realistic characters confronting the moments and details that make up lives and identities.

She lives in the Crowsnest Pass in the Canadian Rocky Mountains with her husband, two dogs, and three cats. She has a B.A. in English and a B.Ed. in English Language Arts Education, and spends most of her time teaching, prepping, marking, and extolling the virtues of Shakespeare. When she isn't doing that, she's usually reading, and when she isn't doing that, she's writing.

To Air the Laundry is her second novel. The Girl with the Empty Suitcase, in which we first meet Sharon through her daughter, Danielle, was her highly-reviewed debut.

You can connect with Krysta via her website or social media.

Website: krystamacdonald.wixsite.com/website
Amazon: amazon.com/author/krystamacdonald
Goodreads: goodreads.com/KrystaMacDonald
Facebook: facebook.com/krystamac.writer
Twitter: twitter.com/KrystaMacWrites
Instagram: www.instagram.com/krysta.macdonald

PRAISE FOR
THE GIRL WITH THE EMPTY SUITCASE

"This book made me laugh. It also made me cry significantly more than I anticipated. The pages of "The Girl With The Empty Suitcase" contained a real mug-shot of marriage, both the highs and potential lows and loneliness. It was a realistic, poignant and often relatable story. I'm highly anticipating Krysta MacDonald's next book!" (Goodreads review)

"This is a really charming book with an interesting central premise. Highly recommended!" (Caryn Lix, author of *Sanctuary* and *Containment*)

"Towards the end of her life, Danielle reflected, "When I was a kid I always thought there would be some moment when I would realize I was an adult, some magical time when I'd feel all grown up, when I'd have all the answers." Neither Danielle nor her creator, Krysta MacDonald, had all the answers, but MacDonald made Danielle real and she made me care about her." (Merilyn Liddell, author of *Tomorrow*).

"A beautifully honest story of two lives intertwining through the very relatable obstacles of life! A lovely debut novel for the author :)" (Goodreads review)

"Krysta MacDonald observes the connection of people. As the reader gets to know Danielle and Mark through their relationship, we identify struggles and the challenges of living up to our own assumptions. This could also be a good reminder to select what baggage we really want to hoist through life. Life is a boundless journey. Pack well." (Goodreads review)

"What a delightful read! An inventive format that is easy to read and propels you forward wanting to know the next stage of 'her' life. Perfectly voiced for every age and renders memories of the readers own life at those ages. Full of surprises, emotion and love. I highly recommend this book." (Many Eve-Barnett, author of *The Rython Kingdom, The Twesome Loop, Clickety Click,* and *Life in Slake Patch*)

"Danielle and Mark alternate telling their tale over the course of forty years, from childhood, before they meet, to old age, after one of them has passed. Together and separately, they grapple to balance life goals, career, family expectations and affection. It is not a particularly colorful tale; rather, it is muted and understated. The sentences are short. The characters struggle to find words for their feelings; they come out sideways. Far from a fairy-tale romance, this book still conveys a heroic and enduring love. I was inspired by this down-to-earth, relate-able couple and MacDonald's care for them." (from Mari's Book Reviews)

"It was very easy to become emotionally invested in the characters, even though you only get to understand them through specific points of time in their lives. They say you can be defined by the moments in your life, and the author did a very good job defining her characters through the "snapshots" of their lives (pun intended!) Some moments were subtle, others were impactful, but both were combined in a way that created a honest, relatable story of love, loss, and self. A great debut novel!" (Goodreads review)

KRYSTA MACDONALD

EARLY PRAISE FOR
TO AIR THE LAUNDRY

"As understated as quiet Sharon, the writing conveys the power of suppression. It becomes a force larger than her life, reaching out of the book to touch our pasts, our secrets [...] Sharon's character development is rich and layered. On one hand, she is a model wife to whom her husband looks forward to returning every evening. On the other hand, she is intrigued with the hippie culture of her time. [...] In the end, with subtle bravery, she adds up the pieces of her life and chooses her own path. A literary historical fiction, To Air the Laundry conveys with sensitivity and grace a struggle common to many women, through one woman's experience."

- from Mari's Book Reviews

36787140R00110

Made in the USA
San Bernardino, CA
27 May 2019